ORPHAN'S
AWAKENING

By

Jared Cubbage

DEDICATION

I dedicate this book and my love of reading to my mother, who introduced me to the joys that could be found from the simple turn of a page.

ACKNOWLEDGMENT

Not enough can be said about the wonderful family and friends who have pushed me over the years. All of the times I doubted myself on even being able to accomplish such tasks as this, they encouraged me even harder to continue on. No amount of appreciation will be enough for all the support they have shared with me.

ABOUT THE AUTHOR

Not much to say about myself. I am an individual with mostly a country upbringing. I have enjoyed reading over the years and would write in my spare time throughout my adult years. I used reading as mostly a way to dive into new worlds with all the different possibilities. My inspiration to write this book stemmed from my family asking me to write stories for my nieces and nephews.

AUTHOR'S NOTE

To the lost children, the forgotten souls, and the hidden heirs of every tale. May you find the courage to embrace the lineage whispered in your blood, the magic dormant within your spirit, and the destiny that awaits beyond the shadows of your past. For in every orphan's heart beats the potential for greatness, a legacy waiting to be reclaimed, and a world eager for the light you carry. This story is for you, a testament to the strength found in uncovering your truth, even when that truth is veiled in mystery and guarded by ancient powers. May your journey be as filled with wonder and discovery as Elara's, and may you always remember that even the quietest whisper can ignite a roaring flame. To those who feel the call of the unknown, the pull of ancestral echoes, and the burgeoning power within – this is your adventure. Embrace it.

CONTENTS

CHAPTER 1:

WHISPERS OF THE FORGOTTEN

The biting winds of the Northern Marches were as constant as the gnawing emptiness in Elara's chest. They howled around the Graystone Orphanage, a hulking edifice of grim stone that seemed to absorb all warmth and light. For as long as her memories stretched, Graystone had been her world—a world of echoing corridors, scratchy wool blankets, and the ever-present scent of damp stone and boiled cabbage. Life here was a meticulously orchestrated monotony, a grey tapestry woven from the threads of daily chores and hushed whispers. Each day dawned indistinguishable from the last, a slow, predictable march of hours punctuated only by the mournful toll of the chapel bell or the rustle of starched uniforms.

Elara, a creature of quiet corners and watchful silences, found her only respite in the orphanage's neglected library. Dust motes danced in the slivers of weak sunlight that pierced the grimy windowpanes, illuminating stacks of ancient tomes that smelled of forgotten spells and faded ink. These books were her windows to worlds beyond the imposing stone walls of Graystone, her escape from the pervasive sense of being adrift. She devoured tales of faraway lands, of brave knights and cunning sorceresses, of creatures that soared through star-dusted skies and swam in sapphire seas. In their pages, she could be anyone, go anywhere, a stark contrast to the solitary, unremarkable orphan she was in reality.

The deepest ache within her, however, was not for grand adventures, but for a past she could not recall. The absence of her parents was a void that no amount of fabricated lore or whispered bedtime stories could fill. It was a phantom limb, a constant, dull throb that underscored her every waking moment. She was a leaf torn from its tree, buffeted by winds she didn't understand, with no roots to anchor her, no memories to guide her. This gnawing melancholy, this persistent feeling of being utterly alone, permeated her very being, making her feel like a ghost in her own life. The pervasive gloom of Graystone, with its shadowed hallways and perpetually overcast skies, was a physical manifestation of the unanswered questions that clung to her like a shroud. Who were her parents? Why had she been left at Graystone? Was there anyone in the world who remembered her, who longed for her? These were the whispers that haunted her, the forgotten echoes of a life lost before it had truly begun.

The days blurred into a single, unbroken expanse of gray. Elara would rise with the sun, a pale imitation of the star it was, and begin her duties. There were floors to be scrubbed until her knuckles were raw, linens to be mended with painstaking stitches, and vegetables to be peeled for the evening meal. The Matron, a woman whose face seemed permanently set in a grimace of disapproval, ruled the orphanage with an iron fist clad in a velvet glove, though the velvet was worn thin with age and overuse. Her pronouncements were delivered in a clipped, severe tone that left no room for argument or complaint. Elara, naturally compliant and disinclined to draw attention to herself, performed her tasks with quiet efficiency, her thoughts miles away, lost in the pages of a borrowed book or the phantom landscapes of her imagination.

She watched the other children, a motley collection of lost souls, with a detached curiosity. Some clung to each other for comfort, forming fragile alliances against the harsh realities of their existence. Others, hardened by their experiences, developed a boisterous, defiant spirit, their laughter echoing with a hollow desperation. Elara remained on the periphery, an observer rather than a participant. Her quiet nature was often mistaken for timidity, her introspection for aloofness. She longed, in the secret chambers of her heart, for connection, but the fear of rejection, of being found wanting, kept her walled off, a fortress of one.

The library was her sanctuary, a dimly lit haven where the scent of aged paper and leather soothed her restless spirit. She would spend hours there, tracing the intricate illustrations of mythical beasts, poring over maps of kingdoms that existed only in ink and imagination, and losing herself in the lyrical prose of poets long dead. She felt a kinship with the forgotten stories, with the tales of individuals who, like her, felt out of place, who yearned for something more. The books offered a silent companionship, a testament to the enduring power of words and the human desire to create meaning in a chaotic world. She would often read passages aloud in a hushed whisper, the ancient words resonating in the quiet air, a secret communion between her and the ghosts of authors past.

One particular book, bound in dark, scuffed leather with no title on its spine, held a peculiar fascination for her. Its pages were filled with cryptic symbols and elegantly rendered drawings of celestial bodies and strange, geometric patterns. It spoke of ley lines, of earth energies, and of the subtle currents that flowed beneath the surface of reality, forces that could be harnessed by those with the understanding to perceive them. Elara found herself drawn to these concepts, feeling an inexplicable resonance with the text, as if it were speaking a language she almost, but not quite, understood. She would pore over the symbols, her fingers tracing their forms, a strange tingle running through her fingertips. It felt as though the book held secrets, not just about the world, but about herself, secrets that lay dormant, waiting to be awakened.

The pervasive gloom of Graystone was a physical weight, a constant reminder of her unanswered questions. The orphanage, perched on a windswept rise in the Northern Marches, was a place that seemed designed to foster despair. Its stark stone walls rose like ramparts against the relentless elements, and the perpetual mist that clung to the surrounding moors seemed to seep into the very marrow of its inhabitants. Elara often found herself staring out of the grimy windowpanes, her gaze lost in the swirling grey, wondering if the mist that obscured the horizon was a reflection of the fog that enshrouded her own past. The silence within the orphanage was not a peaceful silence, but a heavy, expectant one, as if the very stones were holding their breath, waiting for something that would never come.

She would trace the patterns of condensation on the glass, her breath fogging the pane, and imagine herself somewhere else, anywhere else. Sometimes, she envisioned a sun-drenched land, a place of vibrant colors and laughing people. Other times, she saw a place of profound stillness, a vast, silent forest where ancient trees whispered secrets to the wind. These daydreams were her only true solace, brief respites from the relentless grey of her reality. They were fleeting, ephemeral, like the mist outside, always dissipating, always leaving her with the same gnawing emptiness. Yet, she clung to them, for they were all she had of a world beyond Graystone, of a life she yearned for but could not articulate.

The absence of any memento, any tangible link to her origins, was a constant source of pain. The other children often spoke of families, of visits from relatives, of letters that brought news from the outside world. Elara had nothing. She was a blank slate, an unwritten story, and the uncertainty was a torment. She would sometimes clasp her hands together, fingers interlaced, as if by some act of sheer will she could conjure a memory, a face, a name. But there was only the smooth, unblemished skin of her own hands, and the cold, hard reality of Graystone.

She remembered, with a clarity that was both comforting and agonizing, the one small, tarnished silver locket that had been tucked into the swaddling clothes she had arrived in. It was her only possession, a silent testament to a past shrouded in mystery. The matron had kept it locked away, deeming it too precious, or perhaps too significant, to be entrusted to a child. But Elara had seen it, glimpsed its intricate carvings, and felt a strange, humming warmth emanating from it, even through the glass of the matron's desk drawer. It was a flicker of hope in the overwhelming darkness, a symbol of a connection, however tenuous, to the unknown figures who had brought her here. She would often touch the space on her chest where the locket might have rested, a phantom weight, a silent prayer for answers. The unadorned simplicity of her life in Graystone was a stark contrast to the intricate carvings she imagined on the locket, a contrast that mirrored the vast chasm between her current existence and the unknown heritage that whispered to her in her dreams. The unanswered questions were not just abstract thoughts; they were a tangible presence, a heavy cloak that she could not shed. The gloom of Graystone was not merely atmospheric; it was a reflection of the internal landscape of an orphan searching for herself in a world that offered no clues.

The air in the Northern Marches, even at the cusp of evening, retained a frigid bite, a testament to the encroaching autumn. Elara, accustomed to the biting winds that often whipped through the meager herb garden behind Graystone Orphanage, found herself unusually sensitive to the chill that settled over her this particular twilight. She was meticulously tending to the wilting sprigs of rosemary and thyme, her fingers, roughened by countless chores, gently coaxing a few last drops of life from the hardy plants. The setting sun bled across the bruised-purple sky, casting long, distorted shadows that stretched and writhed across the cobblestone courtyard, transforming familiar shapes into something spectral. The usual symphony of Graystone's evening routine – the clatter of pots from the kitchen, the distant murmur of children's voices, the mournful toll of the chapel bell signifying supper – seemed muted, almost distant, as if the world outside the orphanage walls had paused to hold its breath.

It was in this hushed interlude, as the last vestiges of daylight surrendered to the deepening gloom, that she first perceived him. He emerged not from the main gate, nor from the winding path that led to the orphanage's back entrance, but as if coalesced from the very shadows that were then engulfing the courtyard. One moment, the space by the ancient, gnarled oak was empty, save for the creeping tendrils of darkness; the next, a figure stood there, cloaked and utterly still. He was a stark anomaly, a disruption in the predictable rhythm of Elara's life. The fabric of his cloak seemed to drink the fading light, a deep, inky black that offered no hint of its texture or form, only an impression of immense depth. The hood was pulled low, obscuring his face, yet Elara felt, with an unnerving certainty, that she was being observed.

A subtle, almost imperceptible shift in the air preceded his full materialization. It was a prickling sensation that crept across her skin, raising the fine hairs on her arms and the nape of her neck. It wasn't the cold; this was different. It was a low hum, a thrumming beneath the surface of reality, like the resonant vibration of a plucked lute string that Elara couldn't quite hear, but could feel in her bones. It spoke of something ancient, something potent, a power that existed beyond the understanding of the world she knew, a world defined by drudgery and unspoken sorrows. The air around him felt charged, heavy with an unspoken presence that made the very stones of Graystone seem to pulse with a borrowed energy.

The stranger's stillness was profound, unnerving. He didn't move, didn't make a sound, yet his presence dominated the courtyard. He was an island of absolute quiet in the slowly fading cacophony of the evening. Elara, frozen mid-motion with a sprig of thyme in her hand, found herself unable to look away. Her heart, usually a steady, subdued rhythm within her chest, began to beat with a frantic, irregular cadence. She felt exposed, as if this silent observer could see through the worn fabric of her grey uniform, through the layers of dust and grime that clung to her, and into the very core of her being. He seemed to possess an unnerving grace, even in his immobility, a fluid poise that hinted at capabilities far beyond the ordinary.

Slowly, deliberately, the stranger raised a hand, not in greeting, nor in threat, but as if to brush away an invisible mote of dust from his cloak. The gesture, though small, was imbued with a strange significance. As his hand moved, a sliver of moonlight, which had just begun to pierce the thickening clouds, caught the edge of his hood, revealing, for a fleeting instant, the glint of an eye. It was an eye that seemed ancient, sharp, and impossibly deep, like pools reflecting a starlit sky. It held a knowing intensity, a gaze that seemed to pierce through the mundane facade of Elara's carefully constructed anonymity. It was a look that suggested he saw not merely the orphan girl, hunched over dying herbs, but a flicker of something far greater, something buried deep within her, something he had perhaps been searching for.

The prickling sensation intensified, morphing into a tangible aura of awareness. Elara felt an almost overwhelming urge to flee, to retreat into the familiar, if bleak, confines of the orphanage. Yet, her feet remained rooted to the spot. It was as if an invisible tether had bound her to the stranger's presence, an unwilling participant in whatever strange drama was unfolding. The herbs in her hand felt suddenly alien, their earthy scent lost in the palpable charge that permeated the air. She clutched them tighter, a subconscious attempt to ground herself, to anchor herself to the tangible reality of the garden, to anything that wasn't this unsettling apparition.

The stranger's gaze, though unseen from beneath his hood, felt like a physical weight upon her. It was not the casual glance of a passerby, nor the scrutinizing eye of the Matron. This was a gaze that cataloged, that assessed, that seemed to weigh her very essence. He was observing her with an intensity that suggested a deep, underlying purpose. He wasn't simply looking at her; he was *seeing* her, in a way no one ever had. He saw beyond the matted hair, the threadbare dress, the quiet resignation that had become her default setting. He saw, or perhaps sensed, the questions that burned within her, the yearning for a past she couldn't recall, the unspoken longing for a life beyond Graystone's stone walls. It was as if he were privy to the secret whispers of her heart, the silent dialogues she held with herself in the dead of night.

A shiver, entirely unrelated to the temperature, traced its way down her spine. This was not a ghost, not in the way the older children whispered about within the orphanage's shadowed halls. This was something else entirely. This was a presence that felt solid, real, yet imbued with an undeniable aura of the otherworldly. The stranger's arrival was not an accident; it was an event. It was a ripple in the placid, albeit murky, waters of her existence.

As if sensing her internal turmoil, the stranger took a single, deliberate step forward. The movement was silent, fluid, almost predatory. His cloak shifted, revealing a hint of the form beneath, a lean build that suggested agility rather than brute strength. He stopped a few paces away, his stillness returning, but now it felt less like passive observation and more like a coiled tension, a predator waiting for the opportune moment. Elara could feel the subtle shift in his focus, the way his unseen gaze seemed to settle upon her with renewed intensity. It was as if he were waiting for her to acknowledge him, to break the silent tableau.

Her mind raced, desperately searching for an explanation, for a precedent. Was he a relative? A distant cousin came to claim her? But the stern pronouncements of the Matron about her lack of any known kin echoed in her memory. A benefactor? Graystone rarely received visitors of such an enigmatic nature. The orphanage's existence was meant to be forgotten, tucked away in the harsh embrace of the Northern Marches. This stranger, with his cloaked presence and the strange hum of power that seemed to emanate from him, felt like a breach in that carefully maintained obscurity.

He remained silent, an enigmatic sentinel against the fading light. The courtyard, usually a place of routine and familiar sounds, had become a stage for something unknown. The shadows deepened, coalescing around him, making him seem to blend with the encroaching night. Elara's breath hitched in her throat. She felt a strange mixture of fear and an undeniable, burgeoning curiosity. This encounter, she knew with a certainty that resonated deeper than any logical thought, was not going to be brief. It was a turning point, a precipice. The carefully constructed walls of her ordinary life were beginning to tremble, and the stranger, cloaked and silent, was the force that threatened to bring them down.

The herbs in her hand felt insignificant now, their medicinal properties a pale imitation of the potent energy radiating from the man before her. She could almost feel it, a tangible force pushing against her senses, a subtle pressure that made her head swim. It was the feeling one might get standing too close to a forge, a radiant heat that wasn't physical but something more elemental. He was a disruption, a question mark etched against the twilight sky, and Elara, the orphan girl who spent her days lost in books and her nights dreaming of a past she couldn't grasp, felt an inexplicable pull towards him. The stranger's eyes, though hidden, felt fixed upon her, and in their unseen depths, she sensed a recognition, a resonance that stirred something ancient and dormant within her own soul. He was a shadow, yes, but a shadow that promised to cast a light, however strange and unexpected, upon the forgotten corners of her existence.

He finally moved, a subtle inclination of his head that somehow conveyed a question, an invitation to speak. The silence stretched, taut and expectant. Elara's voice, when it finally came, was a reedy whisper, barely audible above the rustle of leaves in the ancient oak. "Who are you?"

The words hung in the air, fragile and uncertain. The stranger offered no immediate reply. Instead, he tilted his head slightly, as if considering the question, or perhaps the questioner. The faint moonlight, now stronger as the last of the sun's glow faded, seemed to trace the edge of his hood, hinting at the sharp, angular lines of a face hidden within. Elara felt a tremor of something akin to anticipation. This was it, she sensed. The moment when the whispers of the forgotten might finally begin to take form, when the silence of her past might finally be broken. The stranger's very presence was a testament to a world beyond Graystone, a world of secrets and perhaps, just perhaps, of answers. He was a shadow in the courtyard, yes, but a shadow that was undeniably, profoundly real, and his arrival was the first tangible thread in the unraveling tapestry of her life.

The silence that followed her question was not empty but filled with a subtle, almost musical resonance. It was the sound of unseen forces at play, of energies gathering. Elara found herself studying the stranger's posture, the subtle tension in his shoulders, the way his hands, gloved in dark leather, remained clasped loosely before him. He seemed to embody a controlled power, a stillness that was not born of apathy but of immense, contained strength. It was this controlled energy that fascinated her, that made her heart beat faster, that made her forget the chill in the air and the impending supper call. He was a living enigma, a puzzle presented on a platter of twilight and shadow.

He shifted again, a barely perceptible movement of his weight, and Elara felt a renewed surge of that strange prickling sensation, stronger this time. It was as if the air itself were a conductor, and the stranger, a powerful source of current. She found herself wanting to ask more, to pry at the edges of his mystery, but the words seemed to stick in her throat, clogged by a sudden, inexplicable shyness. It was a feeling she rarely experienced, this sudden self-consciousness, this awareness of her own smallness in the face of such an imposing presence.

The stranger's head lifted, and Elara sensed his gaze sweeping across the courtyard, taking in the weathered stone walls, the sparse, struggling greenery, the few windows that glowed with the dim, flickering light of oil lamps. He took it all in with an appraising eye, his silence a stark contrast to the orphanage's usual cacophony. He seemed to be measuring the very essence of Graystone, finding it wanting. Yet, his focus returned to her, sharp and unwavering. It was a gaze that felt both ancient and intensely present, as if he had witnessed the building of these walls, the planting of these herbs, and countless other mundane scenes throughout the ages, all while searching for something – or someone.

"You have a keen sense, child," a voice finally emerged from the depths of his hood. It was a low, resonant baritone, surprisingly warm despite its quiet intensity. It held the cadence of ages, a timbre that suggested wisdom and experience far beyond any mortal man. The sound itself seemed to vibrate with a hidden power, a subtle magic that made the very leaves on the oak tree rustle in response.

Elara blinked, surprised by the directness of his address. Her sense, as he called it, was simply the discomfort she felt at his sudden appearance, the awareness of something out of the ordinary. But he had seen it, recognized it, and named it. "I... I just felt you," she stammered, her voice still a hesitant whisper. "You appeared from nowhere."

A faint smile seemed to touch the unseen corners of his lips. "Nowhere is a relative term, little one. For those who know where to look, and how to step between the folds of the world, even the most solid-seeming walls can be permeable." He gestured vaguely with one gloved hand, not towards the orphanage itself, but towards the space between the visible and the unseen. "Some places are simply denser with the ordinary, making the extraordinary harder to perceive."

His words, though cloaked in metaphor, resonated with the strange texts she had pored over in the orphanage library, the ones that spoke of hidden pathways and energies that flowed beneath the surface of reality. Could this man be one of the practitioners described in those cryptic pages? One who understood the subtle currents he spoke of?

"You are Elara, are you not?" he continued, his voice cutting through her thoughts.

The directness of the question, the fact that he knew her name, sent another tremor through her. She clutched the herbs tighter, her knuckles white. "Yes," she managed, her voice barely a breath. "How did you know?"

"Names carry echoes," he replied cryptically. "Especially names tied to certain... potentials. And yours has been whispered on the winds for a long time." He paused, and Elara felt a renewed intensity in his gaze, a sense that he was peering into the very marrow of her being. "More importantly, it is a name that carries a great deal of forgotten history."

Forgotten history. The words struck a chord deep within her. That was precisely what she yearned for, what ached within her like a phantom limb. The history she couldn't remember, the past that was a blank, aching void. "I don't understand," she whispered, her voice laced with a desperate hope. "I don't remember anything about my family. I was… I was left here."

The stranger took another slow step closer, and this time, Elara did not flinch. Her fear was being steadily eclipsed by a consuming curiosity, a desperate need to understand. His presence, though unsettling, felt less threatening now, more like a harbinger of revelation. "You remember nothing of your parents?" he asked, his voice softening, losing some of its ancient resonance and gaining a touch of something akin to sympathy. "No faces, no names, no lullabies sung in the dark?"

Elara shook her head, a single tear tracing a path down her dusty cheek. The memory of the empty ache, the profound loneliness, was a constant companion. "Nothing. Only... only a locket. They said it was with me when I arrived. But the Matron keeps it locked away."

The stranger's stillness seemed to deepen. He remained silent for a long moment, his obscured face turned towards her, as if absorbing her words, processing their weight. Then, he spoke again, his voice a low rumble. "A locket, you say? Of silver, perhaps? With intricate carvings, depicting… celestial patterns?"

Elara's breath hitched. He described it perfectly, the locket she had only glimpsed once, the one that felt like the only tangible connection to a life that was otherwise lost to her. How could he possibly know? "Yes," she breathed, her voice trembling with a mixture of awe and disbelief. "How could you possibly know that?"

"Because," the stranger said, and for the first time, Elara felt a distinct sense of the power coiling within him, a power that seemed to ripple outwards, making the very shadows around them deepen and swirl, "that locket is a key. And you, Elara, are far more than just an orphan in a forgotten corner of the Northern Marches."

The pronouncement hung in the twilight air, heavy with unspoken implications. The prickling sensation on Elara's skin intensified, no longer just a tingle but a vibrant, humming awareness. It felt as though the world had tilted on its axis, and the solid ground beneath her feet had become a fluid, shifting landscape. The stranger's words were not just words; they were pronouncements, weaving a new reality around her. He saw not just the orphan girl tending to dying herbs; he saw a flicker of something far greater, a potential that had been lying dormant, waiting for a catalyst. And in his shadowed presence, in the echo of his ancient voice, that catalyst had finally arrived. The courtyard of Graystone, usually a place of mundane routine, had become the stage for the unveiling of a destiny, and the stranger, a silent, cloaked figure, was the architect of this profound and terrifying revelation. The whispers of the forgotten were beginning to coalesce, and they were speaking her name.

The stranger's cloaked form seemed to absorb the last vestiges of the dying light as he took another step towards Elara. The air around him thrummed with an almost tangible energy, a low vibration that resonated deep within her bones, far more potent than any chill from the encroaching night. His movement was fluid, unhurried, yet it carried an undeniable sense of purpose, a predator's deliberate advance. Elara, rooted to the spot, felt a strange calm descend, a surrender to the inevitable unfolding of events. The herbs in her hand were forgotten, their wilted leaves a stark contrast to the vibrant, almost electric, aura that now enveloped the stranger.

"You remember nothing of your parents?" he repeated, his voice a low rumble, like distant thunder gathering on the horizon. It wasn't a question born of casual curiosity, but of deep, almost ancient, knowledge. The sound itself seemed to stir the very air, causing the leaves of the gnarled oak to rustle with an unnatural urgency, as if the ancient tree itself were listening. "No faces, no names, no lullabies sung in the dark?"

Elara could only shake her head, a single tear escaping the dust that clung to her lashes, tracing a stark, clean path down her cheek. The ache of her lost lineage, the profound, gnawing emptiness of not knowing where she came from, was a constant companion, a dull throb beneath the surface of her everyday existence. "Nothing," she managed to whisper, her voice a fragile thread against the growing silence. "Only... only a locket. They said it was with me when I arrived. But the Matron keeps it locked away."

The stranger's stillness intensified, becoming a profound, almost statuesque, immobility. His obscured face, hidden deep within the cowl, seemed to turn towards her, an unseen gaze that felt as if it were not merely looking at her, but delving into the very fabric of her being, sifting through the layers of unanswered questions and buried memories. He remained silent for a long moment, the quiet stretching between them, pregnant with unspoken implications. The night, which had been slowly deepening, seemed to pause, holding its breath as if awaiting a revelation of cosmic significance.

Then, he spoke again, his voice a low murmur that seemed to emanate from the very depths of the shadows that clung to him. "A locket, you say? Of silver, perhaps? With intricate carvings, depicting... celestial patterns? Stars, moons, perhaps even the spiraling nebulae that dance in the furthest reaches of the night sky?"

Elara's breath hitched, a sharp intake of air that felt impossibly loud in the charged stillness. He described it with an uncanny precision, the locket she had only glimpsed once, a fleeting image of tarnished silver and otherworldly symbols, a fragile thread connecting her to a life lost in the mists of time. The Matron, a woman of practicality and stern discipline, had deemed it a trinket, a childish bauble, and

14

had locked it away in her strongbox, a place of secrets and forgotten histories, as if even the memory of it was to be suppressed. How could this stranger, this being of shadow and mystery, know of it? How could he possibly describe its intricate, alien beauty?

"Yes," she breathed, her voice trembling with a mixture of awe and disbelieving wonder. The words tumbled out, barely audible, yet imbued with a raw intensity. "How could you possibly know that? No one speaks of it. The Matron..."

The stranger's head tilted slightly, a subtle gesture that somehow conveyed an understanding that transcended mere words. "Because, Elara," he said, and as he spoke, she felt a distinct surge of the power that coiled within him, a force that seemed to ripple outwards, making the very shadows around them deepen and writhe as if alive. It was a power that spoke of ancient forces, of magic that flowed through the veins of the world, unseen and often misunderstood. "That locket is more than mere silver and carvings. It is a key. A conduit. And you, Elara, are far more than just an orphan in a forgotten corner of the Northern Marches."

The pronouncement hung in the twilight air, heavy with unspoken implications. The prickling sensation on Elara's skin intensified, no longer a mere tingle but a vibrant, humming awareness that seemed to connect her to the very essence of the stranger and the strange energy that emanated from him. It felt as though the world had tilted on its axis, the solid ground beneath her feet becoming a fluid, shifting landscape. The stranger's words were not just words; they were pronouncements, weaving a new reality around her, a tapestry of destiny that she had never dared to imagine. He saw not just the orphan girl hunched over dying herbs, but a flicker of something far greater, a potential that had been lying dormant within her, waiting for a catalyst. And in his shadowed presence, in the echo of his ancient voice, that catalyst had finally arrived.

He reached into the voluminous folds of his cloak, his movements smooth and deliberate. The gesture was not one of menace, but of revelation. Elara watched, mesmerized, as his gloved fingers emerged, and in his palm rested a tarnished silver locket. It was unmistakably the one she had glimpsed, the one she had dreamed of, the one that felt like the last vestige of a life she could not recall. It was circular, its surface dulled by time and neglect, yet even in its worn state, the intricate carvings were breathtaking. Swirling patterns that seemed to represent celestial bodies – not just stars and moons, but celestial bodies in motion, in flux, depicting a cosmic dance that Elara had only seen in the most obscure, forbidden texts within the orphanage's dusty library. The symbols were unlike any she had ever encountered, ancient runes interwoven with geometric designs that spoke of a knowledge far beyond human comprehension.

"This," the stranger said, his voice a low, resonant hum that vibrated through the twilight, "is what you possess. And what possesses you, though you do not yet know it."

He held it out to her. Elara hesitated for only a moment, her gaze locked on the artifact that promised answers, that pulsed with an unseen power. Then, with a trembling hand, she reached out and took it. The moment her fingers brushed against the cool, worn silver, a warmth spread through her palm, a surprising, almost startling, sensation. It wasn't the heat of the sun, nor the warmth of a hearth fire, but an internal warmth, a gentle pulse that seemed to emanate from the very core of the locket. It felt alive, a sleeping entity awakened by her touch. A faint, ethereal light, almost imperceptible at first, began to glow from within the intricate carvings, pulsing in time with her own racing heart.

"It… it feels warm," she murmured, her voice thick with wonder.

"It is awake now," the stranger confirmed. "As are you, in a way that matters. This locket is not merely a keepsake, Elara. It is a fragment of your heritage, a vessel containing echoes of your lineage."

He watched her, his unseen gaze intense, as she turned the locket over in her hands. The weight of it felt significant, far more substantial than its size would suggest. It felt ancient, imbued with the weight of centuries. Her fingers traced the celestial patterns, feeling a strange resonance, a sense of familiarity that defied logical explanation. It was as if her hands knew these symbols, had traced them in a forgotten dream, in a life lived long ago.

"My parents?" she whispered, the question fraught with a desperate hope that warred with the ingrained skepticism of her upbringing.

"They are indeed your parents," the stranger confirmed, his voice a low, steady cadence. "And this locket is their legacy to you. A legacy that has been guarded, waiting for the moment when you would be ready to receive it."

Ready. The word echoed in Elara's mind. What did it mean to be ready? Had she been waiting her entire life for this moment, for this stranger, for this locket? The world she knew, the world of Graystone Orphanage, of endless chores and hushed sorrows, seemed to be dissolving around her, replaced by a vast, unknown landscape of magic and mystery.

With a deep breath, Elara's fingers found the small, almost invisible clasp that held the locket shut. It clicked open with a soft, musical sound that seemed to echo in the sudden silence of the courtyard. She held her breath, expecting to see a miniature portrait, a lock of hair, something tangible that would finally give her a face to associate with the void of her past.

But there was no portrait.

Instead, as the locket sprang open, a swirling, iridescent mist rose from within. It was not smoke, nor vapor, but something far more ethereal, more captivating. It shimmered with a thousand colors, blues and greens and purples, interwoven with threads of silver and gold, like a captured nebula or a sliver of a starlit sky. The mist swirled and danced, forming fleeting, abstract shapes that hinted at things Elara could not quite grasp, at realities just beyond her comprehension. It emitted a faint, sweet fragrance, like blooming night flowers and distant, unheard music.

Elara stared, transfixed, her mind struggling to process the impossible sight. This was not what she had expected. It was something stranger, something more profound. The mist pulsed with a gentle, rhythmic glow, and as she gazed into its depths, she felt a strange sensation, a dizzying pull, as if she were being drawn into its swirling core. It was not an unpleasant feeling, but one of profound connection, of recognition on a level deeper than thought.

"What is this?" she breathed, her voice barely a whisper. "It's... It's not a picture."

"No," the stranger said, his voice softer now, almost gentle. "It is not a picture. It is a memory. Or rather, the potential for memory. This is what your parents left you, Elara. A key to unlock the hidden chambers of your own being, a gateway to understanding your true heritage."

He stepped closer, his form still cloaked in shadow, yet his presence now felt less intimidating, more like a guide, a mentor. "This locket is an artifact of your lineage, imbued with the magic of your ancestors. It has remained dormant, its power contained, waiting for the right heir to awaken it. For generations, it has slept, its secrets locked away, its purpose concealed. But now," he gestured to the swirling mist within the locket, "it is stirring. Your touch, your very presence, has begun to awaken its dormant magic."

Elara looked from the swirling mist to the stranger, her mind reeling. Magic. Heritage. Ancestors. These were words from the fantastical tales she devoured in the orphanage library, tales of heroes and sorcerers, of hidden realms and ancient powers. She had always read them with a wistful longing, a sense of detachment, as if they belonged to a world far removed from her own grim reality. Now, it seemed, the fantastical was bleeding into her existence.

"But... what does it do?" she asked, her voice laced with a desperate curiosity. "What is its purpose?"

The stranger's shadowed form seemed to shift, as if gathering himself. "Its purpose," he explained, "is multifaceted. It is a beacon, a means of identification, for those who know what to look for. It is a reservoir of ancestral energy, a source of power that you can learn to draw upon. And most importantly," he paused, and Elara felt a sense of anticipation building within her, a feeling that she was on the precipice of a truth that would fundamentally alter her understanding of herself and the world, "it is a key. A key to understanding who you are, where you come from, and what you are destined to become."

He looked at her, and though his face was still hidden, Elara felt the weight of his gaze, a gaze that seemed to penetrate the mist, to see through her very soul. "Your parents were not ordinary people, Elara. They were individuals of great power and deep knowledge. They knew the dangers that awaited, the shadows that lurked beyond the veil of the mundane world. And they prepared for those dangers, for you. This locket is their testament, their hope, their legacy."

Elara's fingers tightened around the locket. The warmth within it seemed to intensify, the swirling mist casting an ethereal glow upon her face. She felt a strange connection to this artifact, a sense of belonging that she had never experienced before. It was as if a missing piece of herself had finally been found, a void within her soul being slowly, tentatively, filled.

"They... they knew they would not be able to raise me?" she asked, her voice hushed, tinged with a nascent sadness.

"They knew," the stranger confirmed, his voice carrying a somber weight. "And they ensured that you would be protected, that you would have the means to understand your heritage when the time was right. This locket has been waiting for you, Elara. Waiting for the heir who would carry their blood, their spirit, their potential."

He gestured towards the locket with a slow, deliberate movement. "Open it again. Look closely at the mist. Do you feel it? The subtle currents of energy? The faint whispers of forgotten languages?"

Elara did as he instructed. She opened the locket once more, gazing into the mesmerizing, iridescent mist. And this time, she felt it. A subtle vibration, a faint hum that resonated through her fingertips and up her arm. It was like listening to the faintest melody played on an instrument she had never heard before, yet somehow recognized. She focused, trying to discern the whispers, the fleeting impressions that danced at the edge of her perception. It was like trying to catch starlight in her hands, or to decipher the language of dreams.

"I… I think so," she stammered, her eyes wide with concentration. "It's faint. Like a distant echo."

"That is the beginning," the stranger said, a note of satisfaction in his voice. "The echoes of your ancestors, the whispers of your lineage. This locket is not just a physical object, Elara. It is a living artifact, connected to your very essence. As you grow, as you learn, its power will become more apparent. Its purpose will unfold. It is a journey, not a destination. And this," he indicated the locket once more, "is the first step."

He turned to leave, melting back into the deepening twilight as silently and mysteriously as he had arrived. "You will be contacted again," he said, his voice fading with his receding form. "Until then, guard the locket well. It is more precious than you can imagine. For it holds the secrets of your past, and the keys to your future."

And then he was gone, leaving Elara alone in the courtyard, the chill of the night air seeping back into her skin, the scent of rosemary and thyme a distant memory. But she was no longer truly alone. In her hand, she clutched the silver locket, its tarnished surface now glowing with a faint, internal light. Within its depths, the iridescent mist swirled, a captured nebula of mystery and promise. The whispers of the forgotten were no longer distant echoes; they were becoming a part of her, a nascent song stirring within her soul, a song that promised to unravel the deepest secrets of her lineage and guide her towards a destiny she had never dared to dream. The world, it seemed, was far larger and far more magical than she had ever believed, and the locket, warm against her palm, was her first tangible proof.

The stranger's words, delivered in that same resonant baritone, began to paint a tapestry of a past Elara could scarcely comprehend. He spoke not of humble beginnings or unfortunate circumstances, but of a lineage steeped in power and purpose, a bloodline that had once been a cornerstone of a world veiled from the ordinary eyes of the Northern Marches. "Your parents," he stated, his voice a low hum that seemed to vibrate with the very essence of the story he was weaving, "were not of the common stock. They were part of ancient houses, houses that held dominion over realms unseen, their roots intertwined with the very fabric of magic that shapes this world."

Elara's grip tightened on the locket, its warmth a reassuring anchor in the sea of bewildering information. She pictured her parents, not as spectral figures from a forgotten dream, but as vibrant beings, wielding a power that resonated even now, through the silver artifact she held. The stranger's words were like carefully placed stones, building a bridge across the chasm of her ignorance. He spoke of "houses" and "realms," terms that conjured images from the forbidden books in the orphanage library, tales of kingdoms in the clouds and cities hidden beneath the earth.

"These houses," he continued, his gaze, though unseen, felt fixed upon her, "were keepers of arcane knowledge, wielders of elemental forces, and guardians of ancient pacts. They were not merely influential; they were foundational. Their magic flowed through the land, shaping seasons, guiding stars, and weaving destinies. And you, Elara, carry that potent inheritance within you."

The weight of his pronouncement settled upon her, a dizzying sensation that left her breathless. Magic. It was no longer a concept confined to dusty pages or whispered legends. It was a living, breathing reality, a part of her own being. The stranger's words were like seeds planted in fertile ground, beginning to sprout within her heart, pushing through the layers of doubt and fear that had always defined her existence. "My parents... they were powerful?" she managed to ask, the words catching in her throat.

"They were more than powerful, Elara. They were pillars of a society that had long since faded into the annals of forgotten lore. They possessed a profound connection to the primal energies of the world, a gift passed down through countless generations. Their influence stretched far beyond the tangible, touching the ethereal planes and commanding respect from beings that few have ever seen, let alone understood." He paused, as if allowing her to absorb the sheer magnitude of this revelation. "The legacy you bear is not one of mere sentimentality; it is one of immense potential, a power that, in the wrong hands, could be a terrible weapon."

This last statement sent a shiver down Elara's spine. A weapon? The notion was terrifying, yet strangely exhilarating. Her entire life had been spent in the quiet anonymity of the orphanage, where the greatest peril was a misplaced broom or a stern scolding. Now, she was being told that she carried within her a force that could be wielded for great good or profound destruction. The stranger's words were not meant to frighten her, she realized, but to impress upon her the gravity of her heritage.

"For this very reason," he explained, his voice taking on a more somber tone, "your lineage had to be hidden. The world changed, Elara. The age of the great houses waned, and darker forces began to stir. To protect you, to allow you to grow and learn without the shadows of your parents' enemies hunting you, a deliberate veil was cast over your existence. Your parents made great sacrifices, not only for their own people, but for you, their child, to ensure your survival and the eventual blossoming of your own abilities."

Elara's mind raced, piecing together fragments of half-heard conversations, the lingering whispers of the older orphans about mysteriously disappearing children, and the Matron's oft-repeated warnings about straying too far from the orphanage grounds. Had those warnings been more than just pronouncements of authority? Had they been whispers of a hidden danger, a reality she had been too young and too ignorant to perceive?

"The magic within you," the stranger continued, "is not a passive gift. It is a living current, a river of ancestral power that flows through your veins. It is tied to the very essence of your being, to the stars that guided your ancestors and the earth that nourished their domains. Your parents understood this, and they ensured that the means to understand and control this power would be available to you when the time was right." He gestured to the locket again, its gentle glow seeming to pulse in understanding. "This locket is not merely a memento. It is a conduit, a key that can unlock those dormant chambers of your inner self. It resonates with the magic of your bloodline, amplifying what is already within you, guiding you toward its mastery."

He spoke of the "primal energies," of "elemental forces," of "ancient pacts." These were not the fanciful imaginings of children's stories, but the pronouncements of someone who had witnessed, perhaps even wielded, these very forces. Elara felt a burgeoning curiosity, a desire to understand the world her parents had inhabited, the world that was now, it seemed, her own birthright.

"Your parents were not just powerful individuals," he reiterated, "they were integral to the balance of a world that most have forgotten. They stood against encroaching darkness, brokering peace between warring factions and safeguarding ancient secrets. Their actions had repercussions, both positive and negative, that rippled through time, and their legacy, both their triumphs and their burdens, now rests upon your shoulders."

The words "burdens" and "enemies" lingered in the air, heavy with unspoken threats. Elara felt a prickle of apprehension, a cold dread that warred with the burgeoning sense of pride and hope. What kind of enemies had her parents faced? What darkness had they stood against? And more importantly, were those same threats still lurking, waiting for her to emerge from the shadows?

"The matron of the orphanage," the stranger mused, his voice a low murmur, "she knew... or at least suspected. Her keeping the locket locked away was not merely an act of proprietorship; it was an act of protection, a misguided attempt to shield you from a destiny she could not comprehend." He seemed to imply a level of awareness on the Matron's part that Elara had never considered. The stern, unyielding woman who had overseen her meager existence was, perhaps, more than just a guardian of orphans; she was a keeper of secrets, albeit an unwitting one.

"The locket," he continued, "is a key that will not only unlock your own latent abilities but will also serve as a beacon to those who understand its significance. It will draw attention, Elara. Not all of it will be benevolent. But it will also guide you to allies, to those who recognize the ancient symbols etched upon its surface and understand the power it represents."

He spoke of a clandestine network, a hidden society that existed on the fringes of the known world, comprised of individuals who still held onto the old ways, who understood the ebb and flow of magic and the true nature of power. These were the individuals who had kept watch over her, the ones who had ensured her safety from afar, waiting for the moment when she would be ready to reclaim her heritage. Her parents, he explained, had been deeply connected to this network, their actions often coordinating with its members to maintain a fragile peace.

"Your parents' sacrifice," he said, his voice resonating with a deep, almost sorrowful, respect, "was not in vain. They ensured your survival, and in doing so, they preserved a lineage that is vital. The world of magic is not static, Elara. It shifts, it evolves, and sometimes, it falters. Your bloodline carries a specific resonance, a unique gift that is needed now more than ever. The currents of power are shifting, and without those who can harness the old magic, the balance will tip precariously."

Elara's mind struggled to keep pace. She was an orphan, a girl who had spent her life picking weeds and mending clothes. Now, she was being told that she was the descendant of ancient, powerful figures, a bearer of a magical legacy that was crucial to the fate of unseen realms. The fear was still present, a knot in her stomach, but it was being steadily eroded by a growing sense of awe and a dawning realization of her own potential. The locket in her hand felt heavier, imbued with the weight of this extraordinary inheritance.

"This is not a path you have chosen," the stranger acknowledged, as if sensing her inner turmoil. "It is a destiny that has chosen you. Your parents foresaw this. They prepared for it. And they entrusted this locket, this key, to ensure that you would have the means to navigate the challenges that lie ahead. It is a symbol of their love, their foresight, and their unwavering belief in your strength."

He took a step closer, and Elara instinctively flinched, not in fear, but in anticipation. "The path you will walk will be fraught with peril," he warned, his voice softening, "but it will also be illuminated by the wisdom of your ancestors and the inherent power that flows through you. You will learn to decipher the whispers of the locket, to understand the celestial patterns etched upon its surface, and to harness the magic that is your birthright. It will not be an easy journey, but you will not be alone. Those who recognize your lineage, those who share your ancestors' purpose, will find you. And they will guide you."

Elara looked down at the locket again, its faint glow seeming to deepen as if responding to the stranger's words. The swirling mist within pulsed gently, a silent promise of secrets yet to be revealed. The fear was still there, a shadow at the edge of her awareness, but it was now dwarfed by a powerful surge of hope, a burgeoning sense of purpose that had been absent for her entire life. She was no longer just Elara, the orphan of Graystone. She was Elara, the descendant of noble houses, the inheritor of ancient magic, a child of a forgotten lineage, and the locket in her hand was the key that would unlock her destiny. The whispers of the forgotten were growing louder, no longer faint echoes, but a resonant call to a life she had never dared to imagine.

The stranger's words hung in the air, a tangible presence that shifted the very atmosphere of the dimly lit room. Elara felt it – a subtle hum of energy, a resonance that seemed to emanate from the locket itself, now clutched tightly in her hand. It was no longer just a piece of silver warmed by her skin; it was a testament, a key, and now, it seemed, a harbinger. The man before her, his form still indistinct in the swirling mist, was not merely a storyteller or a messenger of her past. He was an architect of her future, a deliberate guide sent to nudge her from the stagnant pond of her current existence into the raging river of a life she had never known.

"The time has come, Elara," his voice, a deep, resonant tide, washed over her, each syllable carefully chosen, each word carrying the weight of ages. "The whispers you have heard, the feelings that stir within you – they are not figments of an overactive imagination. They are the stirrings of your blood, the awakening of your legacy. Graystone has served its purpose. It has been a sanctuary, a place where the shadows of your lineage could not easily find you, where your nascent power could remain hidden, undisturbed. But a sanctuary cannot be a prison forever."

He took a step forward, and though his features remained obscured, Elara felt an undeniable presence, a benevolent strength that pushed back the lingering tendrils of fear. This was not the intimidating power of the orphanage Matron, nor the casual cruelty of some of the older boys. This was something ancient, something that felt as solid and as grounding as the very earth beneath her feet, yet as expansive as the star-dusted canvas of the night sky.

"Your parents," he continued, his voice laced with a profound respect, "were guardians. They stood at the precipice of worlds, holding back forces that would have consumed much of what you hold dear. Their sacrifice was immense, a testament to their love for you and their commitment to the balance of things. But such sacrifices leave ripples, Elara. And those ripples have finally reached your shore. The veil that has protected you thins. The time for hiding is over."

He paused, allowing the enormity of his words to sink in. Elara's breath hitched in her throat. Leave Graystone? The thought was both terrifying and strangely liberating. Graystone, with its worn stone walls, its perpetual scent of woodsmoke and boiled cabbage, its predictable rhythm of chores and meager meals – it was the only world she had ever known. Yet, within its familiar confines, she had always felt a subtle disharmony, a sense of being out of place, a quiet yearning for something more, something she couldn't even name.

"The world beyond these walls," the stranger's voice grew more earnest, "is a tapestry woven with threads of breathtaking wonder and unimaginable peril. It is a realm where the very air hums with magic, where the ancient forces your ancestors commanded are not mere legends, but living currents. You possess that same inheritance, Elara. It lies dormant within you, a sleeping titan waiting for the right moment to awaken. And that moment, child, is now."

He extended a hand, though Elara couldn't see it clearly; she felt a gentle, insistent pull, an unspoken invitation. "You stand at a crossroads. Before you lies the path you have always known, a path of quiet obscurity, of safety within familiar confines. It is a path that will lead you further away from the truth of your being, a gradual fading into the ordinary. The whispers will cease, the locket will grow cold, and the legacy of your parents will remain a forgotten dream."

He drew a breath, and the air seemed to shimmer around him. "Or," his voice softened, becoming a melodic counterpoint to the first, "you can step towards the light. You can embrace the unknown, venture beyond the sheltering walls of Graystone, and seek the truth of who you are. This path is not paved with ease. It is fraught with challenges, with dangers that will test your courage and your spirit. You will encounter those who would seek to exploit your burgeoning power, those who were your parents' enemies. But you will also find allies, individuals who recognize the ancient symbols on your locket, those who understand the significance of your bloodline, those who will guide you and help you unlock the power that is your birthright."

Elara looked down at the locket, its faint glow a tiny beacon in the encroaching darkness of the room. It felt warm, almost alive, pulsing with a gentle rhythm that seemed to echo the beating of her own heart. The stranger's words were not a command, but a profound offering. A choice. Remain a child of Graystone, forever unaware of the vastness that lay just beyond the horizon, or step into a destiny that was both terrifying and undeniably exhilarating.

The image of her parents, once hazy and spectral, began to sharpen in her mind's eye. She saw them not as the quiet, distant figures of her vague memories, but as vibrant beings, their eyes filled with fierce love and a deep, unshakeable resolve. They had made sacrifices for her, he had said. They had ensured her survival. And now, they, or at least their legacy, seemed to be calling her forward.

"The locket," the stranger's voice echoed, pulling her back to the present, "is more than just a memento. It is a key, a compass, and a shield. It resonates with the ancient magic of your lineage, and it will guide you. It will help you understand the celestial etchings, to decipher the whispers of the forgotten, and to harness the primal energies that lie within you. The matron, in her own way, tried to protect you by keeping it hidden, but even the best intentions can sometimes delay the inevitable. Your destiny cannot be contained by stone walls and watchful eyes."

He paused, his unseen gaze seeming to probe the very depths of her being. "What will it be, Elara? Will you remain a shadow, forever a ward of the ordinary, or will you step into the light and become the inheritor of your true name? The choice is yours, but know this: the current of your lineage flows strong. It cannot be denied forever. The world is shifting, and those who carry the old magic are needed. Your awakening is not merely a personal journey; it is a necessity for the balance of realms unseen."

The weight of his words pressed upon her, a thrilling, daunting pressure. She thought of the long days at Graystone, the monotonous routine, the feeling of being perpetually overlooked. Then, she thought of the stranger's descriptions – worlds of wonder, elemental forces, ancient pacts. It was a stark contrast, a chasm between the life she had and the life that was now being offered.

Her fingers tightened around the locket, the cool metal a grounding sensation. She could feel a subtle vibration emanating from it, a faint, almost musical hum that seemed to whisper promises of untold secrets and incredible power. It was a call, undeniable and insistent, to a future that stretched out before her, unknown and yet, strangely, familiar.

"The path ahead will demand courage," the stranger's voice resonated with a gentle authority. "It will require you to shed the skins of who you thought you were and embrace the magnificent, terrifying truth of who you are destined to be. There will be moments of doubt, of fear, where the safety of Graystone will seem like a siren's call. But remember your parents' sacrifice. Remember the power that flows through your veins. And remember that the locket will be your guide, connecting you to the wisdom of your ancestors and the allies who will seek you out."

He took another subtle step, and Elara felt a shift in the air, as if he were preparing to depart, leaving her with this monumental decision. "Do not fear the unknown, Elara. Embrace it. For within the heart of the unknown lies the greatest adventure, and the truest discovery of oneself. The forgotten realms are stirring, and they await the touch of those who carry their ancient magic. They await you."

The room seemed to grow quieter, the ambient sounds of the orphanage fading into a distant hum. The only reality was the stranger's voice, the locket in her hand, and the profound, life-altering choice that lay before her. The comfortable anonymity of her past was fading, replaced by the dazzling, dangerous allure of her true heritage. The whispers of the forgotten were no longer just distant echoes; they were a thunderous roar, a call to arms, a summons to a destiny that pulsed with the very magic of the world. Elara knew, with a certainty that settled deep in her soul, that she could no longer remain a prisoner of the familiar. The light beckoned, and she was ready to step into it, no matter the cost.

CHAPTER 2:

THE AWAKENING SPARK

The air in the Whispering Woods was thick, not with the damp chill of twilight, but with an almost palpable sentience. Above them, the sky bled a deep, unnatural vermilion, the rare crimson moon hanging like a bruised eye, casting an eerie, blood-tinged luminescence upon the gnarled trees that clawed at the heavens. This was no ordinary night. Elara, her heart a frantic hummingbird against her ribs, walked beside Kael, the stranger whose presence had irrevocably fractured her predictable world. His steps were silent, a testament to a life lived in concert with the wild, and his silhouette, stark against the crimson glow, was a comforting anchor in the disorienting beauty of their surroundings.

The woods were aptly named. Every rustle of leaves, every snap of a twig, every mournful sigh of the wind weaving through the ancient canopy seemed to carry a fragment of a secret, a whisper of forgotten lore. The trees themselves were behemoths, their bark like the wrinkled skin of titans, their branches twisted into grotesque, arthritic gestures. Some bore scars that spoke of ancient battles, others seemed to cradle nests of shadow, their interiors impossibly dark. Elara felt a prickling sensation on her skin, as if countless unseen eyes were observing their passage. This was not the passive silence of a familiar forest; this was an active, listening presence. The very soil beneath her worn boots seemed to thrum with a latent energy, a deep, resonant hum that mirrored the unsettling tremor within her own being.

"The Crimson Moon," Kael murmured, his voice a low rumble that seemed to blend with the forest's own chorus, "marks a time of potent transitions. The veil between realms thins, and the echoes of the past are amplified. It stirs what lies dormant, both within the earth and within certain souls." He glanced at Elara, his gaze, though shrouded in the dim light, felt penetrating. "You feel it, don't you? The quickening?"

Elara could only nod, her throat tight. It was more than just a feeling; it was a physical sensation. The energy that had flickered to life with the locket now seemed to surge, responding to the spectral light of the moon and the ancient vitality of the woods. It was an intoxicating, terrifying cocktail of emotions – fear of the unknown, a desperate exhilaration at finally being on a path that felt... right, and a deep, resonating connection to this wild, breathing place. She had always felt an affinity for nature, a quiet comfort in the dappled sunlight of the orphanage garden or the scent of rain on dry earth. But this was different. This was a primal recognition, as if the woods were an extension of herself, and she, a lost child returning home.

Kael led her along a winding path, barely more than a deer trail, that snaked between colossal oaks and ancient pines. His movements were fluid, his awareness of their surroundings absolute. He would pause, a hand raised, and Elara would instinctively halt, sensing an unseen obstacle or a subtle shift in the forest's mood. He navigated fallen logs with effortless grace, skirted around moss-covered boulders that seemed to pulse with their own internal light, and guided her across a babbling brook whose waters reflected the crimson moon like shattered rubies.

"These woods," Kael explained, his voice never rising above the rustling symphony around them, "are a living testament to the Old Ways. They remember the pacts made between mortals and the primal spirits, the songs sung to the earth and sky. The trees here are sentient, in their own way. They absorb the memories of all that transpires beneath their branches. Some are keepers of sorrow, others of joy, and many, like the ancients ahead, are guardians of potent, slumbering magic."

As they ventured deeper, the trees grew even more imposing, their canopies so dense that the crimson moonlight struggled to penetrate, creating a mosaic of deep shadows and pools of unearthly light. Strange flora, unseen in the mundane world outside Graystone's walls, bloomed in the perpetual twilight – phosphorescent fungi that cast an ethereal glow on damp logs, vines that writhed with a slow, deliberate motion, and flowers with petals like spun moonlight, unfurling cautiously in the scarce illumination. The air grew cooler, carrying the scent of damp earth, decaying leaves, and something else... something metallic and wild, like ozone after a lightning strike.

Elara found herself instinctively reaching out, not with her hands, but with an inner sense, a nascent awareness Kael had somehow awakened. She could feel the subtle currents of energy flowing through the woods, like invisible rivers. She could sense the life force of the ancient trees, their slow, deliberate pulse, and the fleeting lives of the woodland creatures, their fear and their curiosity. The locket around her neck, nestled beneath her tunic, pulsed with a steady, comforting warmth, as if harmonizing with the very essence of this place.

"Your lineage," Kael said, his voice soft, as if he could sense her inner explorations, "is deeply intertwined with the natural world, Elara. The power you are beginning to awaken is not alien to you; it is an inheritance, a language your blood remembers, even if your mind has yet to fully comprehend it. The resonance you feel is the echo of your ancestors, who walked these woods when they were wilder still, when the ancient spirits held sway more freely."

He stopped beside a colossal oak, its trunk so wide it would take several men to encircle it. Its bark was a tapestry of moss and ancient runes, glowing faintly with the moon's strange light. The tree seemed to exhale a palpable aura of age and wisdom. Elara felt a profound sense of peace settle over her as she stood in its presence, a stark contrast to the churning unease that had been her constant companion for days.

"This is an Elder Tree," Kael explained, his hand resting gently on its rough surface. "It has stood here for millennia. It has witnessed the rise and fall of empires, the ebb and flow of magic. It is a nexus of the forest's energy. The crimson moon amplifies its connection to the spirit realm, making its whispers clearer to those who can listen."

He looked at Elara, his expression serious. "Try. Focus your intent. Reach out, not with your hand, but with your mind, with your heart. Feel its ancient presence. Do not try to understand, merely to connect."

Elara hesitated, then took a deep breath, the cool, charged air filling her lungs. She closed her eyes, trying to push aside the cacophony of her thoughts and fears. She focused on the warmth of the locket, on the steady beat of her own heart, and on the immense, silent presence before her. Slowly, tentatively, she reached out with that newly discovered inner sense.

At first, there was nothing but a vast, silent hum, like the deep ocean. Then, as she held steady, fragments began to coalesce. Images, not visual in the way she understood sight, but more like impressions, flooded her mind. She felt the slow, patient growth of roots delving deep into the earth, the gentle kiss of sunlight on leaves, the relentless cycle of seasons. She felt the passage of countless years, a slow, unhurried march of time. And then, something more. A sense of deep, quiet sorrow, like a vast, ancient grief that had been absorbed into the very wood of the tree. And beneath that sorrow, a flicker of fierce, protective energy, a steadfast guardian watching over its domain.

She gasped, her eyes flying open. The impression lingered, a phantom sensation that sent a shiver down her spine. "I… I felt it," she stammered, her voice trembling with a mixture of awe and disbelief. "It's… old. And sad, but… strong."

Kael's lips curved into a rare, genuine smile. "You listened. That is the first step. Your capacity to connect with the living magic of this world is strong. It is a gift, and a responsibility." He turned, gesturing further into the deepening woods. "The path ahead is not always so welcoming. The woods hold not only ancient guardians but also shadows that have been drawn by the crimson moon, creatures that thrive in its unholy light. Your ability to feel the forest's pulse will be your greatest defense, and your locket, your guide."

They continued their journey, the crimson moon painting their surroundings in hues of deep crimson and inky black. The whispers of the woods seemed to intensify, no longer just the sounds of wind and leaves, but a murmuring chorus of unseen entities. Elara felt a growing awareness of the subtle shifts in the atmosphere, the sudden stillness that preceded danger, the faint scent of decay that signaled an unwelcome presence. Kael moved with an assuredness that bordered on prescience, anticipating every hidden root, every treacherous dip in the terrain. He seemed to be reading the forest like a book, his knowledge as ancient and profound as the woods themselves.

At one point, they emerged into a small clearing where the crimson moonlight fell in an unbroken pool. In the center stood a cluster of ancient standing stones, etched with symbols Elara vaguely recognized from the locket. The air here was charged, crackling with an almost visible energy.

"These are the Moonstones," Kael explained, his voice hushed with reverence. "They were erected by the First Ones, a place where the terrestrial and celestial planes touch. They amplify the moon's power, drawing down its light and infusing it into the earth. It is a place of power, and of ancient memory."

As Elara stepped closer, she felt a pull, a subtle invitation from the stones themselves. The symbols on her locket seemed to vibrate in response, humming with a faint, resonant energy. She reached out, her fingers hovering just above the cool, smooth surface of one of the stones. As her skin neared it, a faint blue light flared within the crimson glow, tracing the etched symbols. It felt like a greeting, a recognition.

"The markings on your locket," Kael said, his voice low, "are ancient script, a form of primal magic. They speak of your lineage, of your inherent connection to the celestial cycles and the earth's power. These stones acknowledge that connection. They are part of the same ancient tapestry."

Elara felt a wave of emotion wash over her – a sense of belonging, of finally finding pieces of a puzzle she hadn't even known existed. The isolation she had carried for so long, the feeling of being an outsider even in her own skin, began to recede. Here, under the alien glow of the crimson moon, surrounded by the echoes of ancient magic, she felt more at home than she ever had within the stone walls of Graystone.

Their journey was not without its perils. As they navigated a particularly dense thicket, a guttural snarl echoed through the trees. Shadows detached themselves from the deeper darkness, coalescing into vaguely lupine forms with eyes that burned with a malevolent, predatory hunger. These were not ordinary wolves; their forms were distorted, their movements unnaturally swift, and the air around them felt cold and suffocating.

"Gloom Hounds," Kael stated calmly, drawing a slender, wickedly sharp blade from his belt. It seemed to absorb the crimson light, its edges shimmering with an inner power. "Drawn by the moon's intensity and the scent of awakened magic. They are drawn to fear, and to the light they cannot comprehend."

He moved with a speed that Elara could barely follow, his blade a blur of motion. He didn't fight with brute force, but with a precision that seemed to anticipate each lunge, each snap of razor-sharp teeth. Elara, though terrified, felt a surge of something akin to courage.

She gripped the locket tightly, its warmth a small but potent shield against the encroaching darkness. She focused on the energy she felt flowing from the woods, a silent plea for protection.

As Kael engaged the creatures, Elara felt a strange resonance build within her. It was a primal urge, a protective instinct that felt ancient and powerful. She found herself focusing on the Gloom Hounds, not with malice, but with a fierce intent to repel them. She envisioned a wall of light, pushing back against their shadows. It was a fragile attempt, a mere flicker of intent, but surprisingly, the creatures nearest to her recoiled, whimpering as if struck by an unseen force.

Kael noticed. A flicker of surprise, quickly masked, crossed his face before he dispatched the last of the hounds, which dissolved into wisps of acrid smoke. "Well done, Elara," he said, sheathing his blade. "You are learning to wield your connection. The woods responded to your will."

Elara was breathless, her heart still pounding, but a new kind of exhilaration coursed through her veins. She had faced danger, and she had, in a small way, fought back. She had tapped into something within herself, something that resonated with the very life force of the woods. The crimson moon, which had initially felt so foreboding, now seemed like a witness, a celestial amplifier of the magic that was awakening within her.

As they pressed on, the landscape began to shift. The ancient trees gave way to more gnarled, twisted forms, their branches skeletal and claw-like. The air grew heavy, carrying a scent of decay and something metallic, like old blood. The whispers of the woods became more agitated, tinged with a palpable fear.

"We are nearing the heart of the shadowed grove," Kael warned, his voice losing its earlier calm, now laced with a grim watchfulness. "This is where the ancient conflicts left their scars, where the veil is thinnest and the creatures of the night hold sway."

Elara tightened her grip on the locket. The journey through the Whispering Woods had been more than a mere passage; it had been a revelation. She had felt the pulse of a world far grander and more dangerous than she had ever imagined. She had connected with the ancient magic that flowed through her veins, and she had taken her first hesitant steps towards embracing her destiny, all beneath the watchful, crimson eye of the moon. The sanctuary of Graystone felt like a lifetime ago, a dream from which she had finally, irrevocably, awoken. The path ahead was shrouded in mystery and peril, but for the first time in her life, Elara felt the exhilarating thrum of purpose, a spark ignited by the crimson moon and fanned into a flame by the secrets of the Whispering Woods.

A guttural snarl, devoid of any natural animalistic cadence, ripped through the charged silence of the grove. It was a sound that scraped against the very soul, a harbinger of encroaching dread. From the dense, thorny undergrowth, a wave of movement rippled, coalescing into figures that seemed to bleed from the shadows themselves. Not wolves, not in any true sense of the word, but twisted mockeries, their forms elongated and gaunt, their coats the color of deepest midnight, absorbing the faint crimson light rather than reflecting it. Their eyes, the focal point of their terrifying visage, burned with a malevolent, predatory hunger, twin embers of pure, unadulterated malice that pierced the gloom. These were the Gloom Hounds, creatures forged in the crucible of primal fear and the stagnant darkness that clung to this blighted place.

Kael reacted instantly, his movements a blur of practiced efficiency. His hand shot to his side, and the slender, wickedly curved blade he carried was in his grasp, the metal seeming to drink in the strange lunar glow, its edges sharpening with an almost audible hum. But before he could fully engage, before the first of the spectral beasts could launch its assault, Elara felt it – a tremor, not in the earth beneath her feet, but deep within her very being. It was a primal surge, an instinct so ancient and profound it felt like an echo from a forgotten era. Her heart, which had been a frantic flutter against her ribs, suddenly stilled, replaced by a steady, powerful pulse that resonated with an unheard rhythm.

Without conscious volition, her hands rose, not in a gesture of defense, but as if drawn by an unseen force. Her fingers splayed, palms facing the encroaching shadows, and from them, not a whisper, not a spark, but a veritable torrent of pure, incandescent energy erupted. It was a wave of raw, untamed power, chaotic and wild, yet undeniably potent. The light, a searing white that momentarily dwarfed the crimson moon, slammed into the leading edge of the shadow hound pack. The creatures recoiled with yelps that were more agony than sound, their forms flickering and dissolving at the edges as if struck by an invisible, scorching brand. The very air crackled, thick with the scent of ozone and something else... something burning, something that had once been tangible darkness.

Elara gasped, the sudden expulsion of energy leaving her breathless, her arms trembling with the residual force. Her vision swam for a moment, the world reasserting itself in hazy swathes of crimson and the lingering afterimages of her own blinding light. She stared at her hands, then at the retreating, whimpering beasts, her mind struggling to comprehend what had just transpired. This wasn't the subtle resonance she'd felt with the Elder Tree, or the gentle hum of the locket. This was a cataclysm, a violent outpouring of power that had sprung from nowhere and everywhere within her. The magic felt like a part of her, an intrinsic component she had never known existed, yet it was also utterly alien, a force that had seized control and acted independently of her conscious will.

Kael, who had been poised to defend her, now stood frozen, his blade held mid-air, his gaze fixed on Elara with an expression that mingled shock and something akin to awe. The Gloom Hounds, thoroughly disoriented and seemingly in pain, had faltered in their attack, their predatory focus shattered by the unexpected blast. They circled warily, their burning eyes now darting between Elara and Kael, sensing a threat far greater than they had anticipated. The energy radiating from Elara was palpable, a vibrant hum that seemed to push back against the oppressive darkness of the grove.

"What... what was that?" Elara stammered, her voice barely a whisper, her eyes wide with a mixture of terror and bewildered exhilaration. She flexed her fingers, half expecting another uncontrolled eruption, but the energy had receded, leaving behind only a faint tingling sensation and a profound sense of exhaustion. It was as if a dam had burst within her, releasing a flood that had now subsided, leaving the riverbed exposed and vulnerable.

Kael slowly lowered his sword, his intense gaze never leaving her. He took a slow, deliberate breath, his chest rising and falling with a measured cadence. "That," he said, his voice low and measured, yet carrying a weight of profound significance, "was the awakening. The raw, untamed power of your lineage, Elara, unleashed by the confluence of the Crimson Moon, the ancient energies of this grove, and your own inherent magic. It is not just a part of you; it *is* you. A wild, potent force that has lain dormant, waiting for this moment, for this catalyst."

He took a step towards her, his eyes scanning her with an intensity that was both unnerving and oddly reassuring. "You felt it, didn't you? The instinct to protect, to repel. It was not a learned response; it was a primal command from your very soul. You did not consciously command the energy; it responded to your intent, to your will to preserve yourself, to push back against the darkness that sought to consume you." He gestured towards the lingering Gloom Hounds, who were now beginning to regroup at the edge of the clearing, their initial courage replaced by a cautious fear. "They are creatures born of fear and shadow. Your light, your raw power, was anathema to them. It burned them, physically and spiritually."

Elara's mind reeled. The predictable, ordered world she had known within the sterile walls of Graystone felt a million miles away. This was a reality steeped in magic, in forces she could barely comprehend, let alone control. She had always been a creature of quiet observation, of internal contemplation, never one for grand displays or overwhelming power. Yet, here she stood, the residual energy of her own unleashed magic still humming in the air around her, a testament to a hidden wellspring of power she had never suspected.

The Gloom Hounds, emboldened by the temporary retreat of Elara's energy, began to advance again, their snarls low and menacing. But this time, there was a hesitation in their movements, a wariness born from their previous encounter. They knew the source of the pain, the blinding light, and they were no longer entirely confident in their assault.

Kael's focus shifted back to the immediate threat. "The initial shock is over," he said, his voice regaining its firm, steady tone. "They will regroup, and their fear may turn to desperation. You need to control this power, Elara. You cannot afford to be overwhelmed by it, nor can you afford to let it overwhelm them. Think of the Elder Tree, its quiet strength, its deep roots. Feel that steadiness within yourself."

Elara nodded, her eyes fixed on the advancing hounds. She tried to recall the feeling of connection to the Elder Tree, the sense of ancient, unwavering presence. She focused on her breath, trying to find a rhythm that mirrored the steady beat of her heart. She closed her eyes for a fleeting moment, picturing the locket warming against her skin, a tangible anchor in this sea of overwhelming power.

When she opened her eyes, the Gloom Hounds were closer, their spectral forms more defined in the crimson moonlight. She felt the surge of primal fear again, the instinct to lash out. But this time, she tried to temper it with Kael's advice, with the memory of the Elder Tree's steadfastness. She didn't raise her hands wildly; instead, she focused her intent, visualizing a barrier, not of explosive force, but of pure, unwavering light. She imagined it forming around her and Kael, a shield that would absorb their malice, their shadowy essence.

A soft, steady glow emanated from her fingertips, not the blinding torrent of before, but a contained, radiant aura. It spread outwards, forming a shimmering dome of light that pulsed with a gentle, yet insistent energy. The Gloom Hounds halted abruptly, snarling in frustration as their path was blocked. They lunged at the barrier, their shadowy forms meeting with a soft thud that sent ripples through the light. They recoiled, hissing, the pure energy of the shield a tangible, painful barrier against their dark nature.

Kael watched with keen interest, a grim satisfaction playing on his lips. "Good," he murmured, almost to himself. "You are learning. You are channeling. That is the key, Elara. Not suppression, but direction. The power is yours to command, not to be commanded by."

He moved with renewed purpose, his sword flashing in the ambient light. He didn't need to unleash a barrage of attacks; the shield Elara had created was containing the creatures, limiting their avenues of attack. He moved with precise, economical strikes, parrying their lunges, capitalizing on their hesitations, and driving them back. Each movement was a testament to years of training, to a mastery of combat that bordered on the supernatural.

Elara maintained her focus, the effort of sustaining the shield draining her, but also solidifying her control. She could feel the energy flowing through her, a constant, vibrant current that she was learning to guide, to shape. It was exhausting, demanding a level of concentration she had never before been required to exert. But with each passing moment, the alien nature of the magic began to recede, replaced by a growing sense of ownership. This was her power, her birthright, and she was beginning to understand its language.

The Gloom Hounds, sensing their disadvantage and finding their attacks futile against the radiant shield, began to falter. Their snarls turned to mournful whines, and one by one, they began to retreat, melting back into the oppressive shadows from which they had emerged. The air in the grove, though still heavy with the scent of decay and the lingering tang of spent magic, felt lighter, the immediate threat having dissipated.

Elara slowly lowered her hands, the shimmering dome of light fading as her concentration wavered. The exhaustion hit her like a physical blow, and she stumbled, her knees feeling weak. Kael was instantly at her side, his hand steadying her.

"You did well," he said, his voice softer now, a hint of genuine admiration in his tone. "You faced a primal threat, and you did not succumb to fear. You tapped into the heart of your power, and you controlled it. That is a rare and remarkable feat, especially on your first true awakening."

He glanced around the clearing, his eyes scanning the shadowy fringes where the hounds had disappeared. "They will not return tonight, not in full force. They are creatures of instinct, and they have learned that this place and its inhabitants are not to be trifled with. But the shadow still lingers here, Elara. The crimson moon draws many things from the hidden places of the world."

Elara leaned against him for a moment, catching her breath, the adrenaline slowly draining from her system, leaving behind a profound sense of weariness. She looked at her hands again, no longer with fear, but with a dawning understanding. They were not just the hands of an orphan from Graystone; they were the conduits of a power that had lain dormant for centuries, waiting to be awakened. The raw, untamed surge had been terrifying, chaotic, and utterly overwhelming. But the subsequent control, the ability to shape and direct that energy, even for a brief time, had been exhilarating. It was a glimpse into a future she had never dared to imagine, a destiny far grander and more perilous than she could have ever conceived. The Whispering Woods had not only revealed its secrets to her; it had also revealed the secrets within herself. And the journey, she knew, had only just begun. The spark had ignited, and now, it was her responsibility to learn how to tend the flame.

The residual tremors of Elara's unleashed power still thrummed in the air, a vibrant counterpoint to the oppressive stillness of the Whispering Woods. The Gloom Hounds, remnants of shadow and malice, had retreated, their terrifying presence banished for the moment, but the imprint of their aggression, and more importantly, the echo of Elara's explosive reaction, hung heavy between her and Kael. His gaze, which had softened with a hint of admiration as the creatures dissolved into the encroaching darkness, now sharpened with a renewed, almost urgent intensity. He saw not just the girl who had inadvertently unleashed a tempest, but the nascent vessel of a power that demanded immediate and rigorous guidance.

"That was... significant," Kael stated, his voice a low rumble, devoid of any immediate alarm, yet underscored by a gravity that Elara understood far too well. He moved with a practiced grace, his gaze sweeping over the now-empty clearing, his senses clearly still attuned to the subtle shifts and whispers of the woods. "The Crimson Moon amplifies such energies, and this place, these ancient woods, they resonate with power. But what you possess, Elara, is far more than a mere reaction to external stimuli. It is an inheritance."

He turned back to her, his expression earnest. "What you felt, what you *did*, was the awakening of your lineage. A torrent of raw, untamed magic that has lain dormant within you, waiting for a catalyst. The danger, the proximity to such primal fear, and yes," he glanced at the locket still nestled against her collarbone, its faint warmth a ghost of its recent fervor, "the artifact you wear, all conspired to break the dam. It is not something you learned; it is something you *are*."

Elara's breath hitched. Her mind, still reeling from the experience, struggled to reconcile Kael's words with the overwhelming reality of what had just happened. She had always known herself to be ordinary, a mere orphan from the grey, disciplined halls of Graystone Academy. Magic, if it existed at all, was the domain of distant legends and whispered tales, not of her own hands. Yet, the tingling sensation that still lingered in her fingertips, the profound exhaustion that settled deep in her bones, were undeniable proof. "My lineage?" she managed to croak, the words feeling foreign and presumptuous on her tongue.

"Indeed," Kael confirmed, his gaze unwavering. "The power you wield is not a common one. It is tied to an ancient bloodline, one that has long been intertwined with the elemental forces of this world. You felt the instinct, the primal need to protect. That is the first hallmark of your heritage. This power, however, is like a wild horse, Elara. Untamed, it can be a danger to yourself and others. Properly guided, it can be a force of immense creation and protection."

He took a step closer, his presence commanding yet not intimidating. "This is why our journey cannot simply be about reaching your destination. It must also be about understanding and mastering what lies within you. The Gloom Hounds were a violent awakening, a harsh lesson. But we cannot afford to have you react so... explosively... every time your life is threatened. Discipline, control, and understanding are paramount."

Elara's heart hammered against her ribs, a nervous rhythm that felt entirely at odds with the deep calm she had managed to evoke moments before. The thought of more danger, more uncontrolled outbursts, sent a shiver down her spine. But Kael's calm, steady demeanor was a grounding force. He spoke of her lineage not with fanfare or a sense of superiority, but with a quiet understanding of its implications, both its potential and its perils.

"So, what now?" she asked, her voice barely above a whisper, her gaze falling to her trembling hands. They felt both alien and intimately familiar, a source of both terror and a strange, burgeoning pride.

Kael's lips curved into a faint, almost imperceptible smile. "Now, the tutelage begins. The Gloom Hounds have served their purpose, albeit unintentionally. They have shown you the raw power, and they have shown us the urgency. We will not be able to travel with such a potent, uncontrolled force. Every shadow, every rustle of leaves, could trigger another surge, potentially harming us, or attracting far worse than hounds."

He gestured towards a small, relatively clear patch of ground a few yards away from the base of the ancient oak, its gnarled branches reaching towards the crimson sky like skeletal fingers. "We will start here, beneath the watchful eyes of these old woods. Your first lesson is not in conjuring fire or manipulating the earth, but in focus. In intent."

He sat down, cross-legged, his movements fluid and economical. He gestured for Elara to do the same. Hesitantly, she complied, the damp earth seeping through her worn trousers. The exhaustion was still a heavy cloak, but a new feeling was beginning to bloom within her: a fierce determination. She had tasted power, and she had been terrified, but she had also seen its potential, its ability to ward off the encroaching darkness. She would not shy away from it.

"Close your eyes, Elara," Kael instructed, his voice soft but firm. "Breathe. Feel the air enter your lungs. Feel it leave. Do not focus on the sounds of the woods, not yet. Focus on the rhythm of your own breath. The steady beat of your heart."

Elara obeyed, her eyelids falling shut. The cacophony of the Whispering Woods, which had seemed so overwhelming moments before, began to recede, replaced by the quiet cadence of her own breathing. In, out. In, out. Her heart, which had pounded with a frantic urgency, was gradually finding a more measured pace, a steady drum against the silence.

"Now," Kael continued, his voice a low murmur, "try to find that feeling again. Not the explosion, not the torrent. But the *intent*. The desire to push back. The will to create that shield. It was there before, instinctively. Now, you must try to summon it deliberately.

Think of the light you created, the warmth. Imagine it gathering within you, at your core. Do not force it. Let it coalesce, like mist gathering in a hollow."

Elara concentrated, her brow furrowed in effort. She tried to recall the sensation, the surge that had originated deep within her. It felt like trying to grasp smoke, elusive and intangible. She focused on the feeling of the locket against her skin, a subtle warmth that seemed to resonate with the fading echo of her power. She pictured the light, a soft, warm glow, not the blinding inferno of before, but a gentle radiance.

Minutes stretched into an eternity. The exhaustion gnawed at her, whispering temptations to simply surrender to sleep. But Kael's presence, a silent, watchful anchor, kept her tethered. She felt a faint tremor within her, a subtle thrumming that was different from the residual exhaustion. It was a nascent spark, a whisper of the power waiting to be coaxed forth.

"It's... there," she breathed, her voice tight with concentration. "A tiny flicker."

"Good," Kael responded, a note of encouragement in his tone. "Do not try to make it a wildfire. Nurture it. Guide it. Imagine it flowing from your hands. Not with force, but with intention. Visualize your palms, and imagine that light gathering there, a contained orb of steady energy. Feel the purpose behind it: defense, not aggression."

Elara focused on her hands, picturing them held out before her, palms facing upwards. She imagined the subtle energy within her being drawn towards them, drawn to the intention of defense. It was like coaxing a shy creature out of hiding, a delicate dance of will and nascent power. Slowly, tentatively, a faint luminescence began to appear around her fingertips, a soft, ethereal glow that pulsed with a gentle rhythm. It was not the overwhelming torrent she had unleashed against the hounds, but a contained, steady beacon.

"You are channeling," Kael said, his voice filled with quiet satisfaction. "You are not merely reacting; you are directing. This is the fundamental principle, Elara. Magic is not a force that controls you; it is a tool that you must learn to wield. It responds to your intent, your focus, your will. The greater your clarity of purpose, the more potent and precise your control will be."

He watched her with an assessing gaze, his eyes missing nothing. "The energy you unleash can manifest in many ways, depending on your emotional state and your conscious intent. When you were in fear, it was a raw, explosive blast. When you focused on defense, on creating a barrier, it became a shield of light. Now, you are consciously channeling it. This is the beginning of true mastery."

The light around her hands strengthened, growing from a faint glow to a discernible orb of soft, warm radiance. It cast a gentle luminescence on their faces, pushing back the encroaching shadows of the woods. Elara felt a profound sense of connection to this light, a sense of it being an extension of herself, rather than an external force. The exhaustion remained, but it was now tempered by a burgeoning sense of accomplishment.

"This is still rudimentary," Kael cautioned, though his eyes held a glint of pride. "You are learning to summon and sustain a basic manifestation of your power. But the deeper currents, the raw potential that erupted earlier, require more. It requires understanding the ebb and flow, the connection to the world around you, and the discipline to bridle its wilder aspects."

He rose to his feet, extending a hand to help her up. The orb of light around her hands pulsed once, then began to fade as her focus wavered slightly with the movement. "Tomorrow, we will delve deeper. We will explore the nature of the energies that course through you, the ways in which your lineage interacts with the world. We will practice focusing your intent on specific targets, on shaping the energy with greater precision. We will work on resilience, on pushing your limits without succumbing to exhaustion or losing control."

Elara took his hand, her own surprisingly steady now. The experience had been terrifying, draining, and utterly transformative. She had faced not only the external threat of the Gloom Hounds but the internal threat of her own uncontrolled power. And she had, with Kael's guidance, begun to navigate that internal landscape.

"It feels... overwhelming," she admitted, her voice laced with honesty. "All of this... power. It's so much more than I ever imagined."

Kael's grip on her hand tightened, a gesture of reassurance. "It is. And it will continue to be. But overwhelm is the enemy of control. You must learn to breathe through the magnitude of it, Elara. To accept it, to understand it, and ultimately, to command it. Think of it not as a burden, but as a responsibility. A birthright that demands diligence and respect."

He released her hand and turned to scan their surroundings once more, his senses still on high alert. "The night is far from over. The Crimson Moon still holds sway, and this forest is a magnet for creatures drawn to its light and the energies it stirs. We must remain vigilant." He looked back at Elara, his expression serious. "But for tonight, you have taken the first, critical step. You have acknowledged the spark, and you have begun to learn how to tend the flame. That is more than many born with your gift ever achieve."

As they continued their trek deeper into the Whispering Woods, Elara walked with a newfound awareness. The rustling leaves, the distant cries of unseen creatures, the very air that seemed to hum with a latent energy – it all felt different now. It was no longer just the environment she inhabited; it was a canvas upon which her own burgeoning power might soon be painted. Kael's tutelage had begun, and with it, a journey that promised to be as perilous as it was profound, a journey into the heart of magic, and into the depths of her own awakened self. The path ahead was uncertain, but for the first time, Elara felt a flicker of something other than fear: a nascent hope, a nascent strength, born from the ashes of her own uncontrolled awakening. The lessons would be arduous, the discipline demanding, but the promise of understanding and control was a beacon in the encroaching darkness.

The locket, a cool, smooth weight against Elara's skin, suddenly pulsed with a warmth that belied its usual comforting chill. It was a subtle shift at first, a gentle thrumming that vibrated through her, a sensation akin to the echo of a struck bell. As she focused on it, trying to decipher the foreign feeling, the intricate, almost alien symbols etched into its surface began to shimmer. Faint lines of inner light, the color of a twilight sky, bloomed within the carvings, casting an ethereal glow that was visible even through the worn leather of her tunic. It was a silent, yet profound, response to the raw magic that had recently surged through her veins, a magic she was only just beginning to comprehend.

Kael, who had been observing her with a quiet intensity, nodded, his gaze fixed on the locket. "It responds," he stated, his voice a low murmur that seemed to vibrate with the same nascent energy Elara was experiencing. "As I suspected. It is not merely a piece of adornment, Elara. It is an artifact of significant power, intrinsically linked to your lineage, and by extension, to you."

He approached her slowly, his movements unhurried, deliberate. His eyes, sharp and discerning, never left the locket as he gestured for her to place her hand over it. "This artifact," he explained, his tone measured, "is an amplifier. It is attuned to the specific resonance of your bloodline, much like a tuning fork vibrates in harmony with its paired counterpart. When your magic stirs, especially with such untamed force, the locket awakens. It seeks to harmonize with that power, to lend its own inherent strength to your efforts."

Elara's fingers, still tingling with the remnants of her earlier exertion, rested on the locket. Beneath her touch, the warmth intensified, and the faint light within the symbols pulsed with a steadier rhythm. It felt... alive. Not in the way a living creature is alive, but with a potent, focused energy that seemed to hum in sympathy with her own internal tremors.

"An amplifier?" Elara whispered, her voice laced with a mixture of awe and apprehension. The idea that this simple locket, a relic from her unknown past, held such a significant role was almost too much to process. She had always seen it as a fragile keepsake, a lonely link to a history she could not recall. Now, it was revealing itself to be something far more profound.

"Indeed," Kael confirmed. "But it is more than just an amplifier. It is also a conduit, a tool to help stabilize and channel the volatile energies that you have only just begun to awaken. Think of your magic as a wild river, Elara. Powerful, capable of immense force, but prone to unpredictable floods and destructive currents. The locket, when properly understood and utilized, can act as a dam, a series of sluice gates, allowing you to direct that river's flow with greater control and less risk of devastation."

He paused, his gaze meeting hers. "It is a rare gift to possess such a potent artifact that so perfectly complements your inherent abilities. Many who awaken to their lineage must forge such tools, or seek out others, a dangerous and time-consuming endeavor. You already possess one."

Elara closed her eyes, trying to fully immerse herself in the sensations emanating from the locket. It was a strange feeling, this newfound connection to an object. Before, it had been a passive presence, a cool weight. Now, it felt like an extension of herself, a resonant chamber that amplified the faint echoes of her power. She could feel its pulse, a steady, rhythmic beat that was distinct from her own heartbeat, yet somehow intrinsically linked to it.

"How... how do I use it?" she asked, her voice barely audible. The raw power that had erupted from her earlier had been terrifying in its wildness. The thought of harnessing it, of directing it with intention, felt like an impossible task.

"You feel it," Kael instructed, his voice soft, yet imbued with a quiet authority. "You learn its rhythm, its pulse. It is a focal point. When you feel the surge of your magic building, when you sense the uncontrolled energy beginning to flare, you draw your attention to the locket. You imagine its warmth, its light, becoming a beacon within you. You focus your intent, your will, through it."

He knelt beside her, his presence grounding and reassuring. "Let us try. Close your eyes again. Breathe deeply. Feel the locket against your skin. Imagine its light, that soft, twilight glow, expanding. Picture it as a steady, unwavering flame, not a wildfire. Now, recall the feeling of wanting to protect yourself, the primal instinct that drove you earlier. Channel that *intent*, but direct it towards the locket. Imagine the energy flowing from your core, being drawn into the locket, and then radiating outwards from it, contained and focused."

Elara closed her eyes, the image of the glowing symbols vivid in her mind. She focused on the warmth, on the steady pulse. She tried to recall the raw, urgent need to defend herself, the desperate instinct to push back the encroaching darkness. It was a difficult feeling to grasp, so intertwined with the fear and panic of the moment. But Kael's words were a lifeline. She pictured the energy within her, not as a chaotic storm, but as a steady stream, flowing towards the locket, which acted as a lens, gathering and focusing that stream.

Slowly, tentatively, she felt a shift. The locket grew warmer, the light within its symbols intensified, blooming into a more radiant glow. It wasn't a surge, not an explosion. It was a controlled release, a gentle hum of power that radiated outwards from her chest. She could feel it, a soft pressure against her skin, a palpable manifestation of her will, channeled through the artifact.

"You are doing it," Kael breathed, a rare note of genuine admiration in his voice. "You are not merely unleashing raw power; you are shaping it. The locket is acting as a governor, a stabilizer. It is helping you to temper the wildness, to imbue it with your conscious intent."

Elara opened her eyes, a sense of wonder washing over her. The glow from the locket was subtle but undeniable, casting a soft luminescence on her hands. She felt a profound sense of connection, not just to her own magic, but to the locket itself. It was no longer just an object; it was a partner, a silent ally in her journey.

"It feels... different," she murmured, her voice still hushed with disbelief. "Less like a storm, more like... a steady current."

"Precisely," Kael said, a faint smile gracing his lips. "That is the essence of control. The locket helps you to find that steady current, to navigate the powerful waters of your lineage. As you grow stronger, as you learn to exert greater conscious will, the locket will unlock deeper reserves of power and offer even finer control. It will become an extension of your own magical essence."

He stood up, extending a hand to help her to her feet. The glow from the locket, though still present, began to dim as Elara's direct focus shifted. "This is just the beginning, Elara. The locket is a tool, but it is you who wields it. You must practice this. When you feel the stirrings of your magic, even the smallest flicker, try to draw upon the locket. Feel its resonance, and channel your intent through it. Imagine it as your anchor, your point of focus in the storm of your own power."

He began to walk, and Elara followed, the locket now a familiar, comforting warmth against her skin. The journey through the Whispering Woods continued, but the oppressive darkness and the lurking fears of the previous encounter seemed to have receded, replaced by a nascent sense of purpose and a growing understanding of the power that lay within her.

"The Crimson Moon plays a significant role in amplifying such energies," Kael continued, his gaze scanning the dense canopy overhead. "It awakens latent abilities, and it can draw creatures of shadow and ill intent. Your power, now awakened, makes you a beacon. The locket, while stabilizing, can also amplify the signal, making you more noticeable to those who hunt such power."

Elara's hand instinctively went to the locket. A beacon? The thought was both exhilarating and terrifying. She had thought the magic was solely about defense, about pushing back danger. Now, Kael was suggesting it also made her a target.

"So, the locket makes me more powerful," she stated, trying to mask the tremor of unease in her voice, "but it also makes me more visible?"

"It amplifies your inherent resonance, yes," Kael confirmed. "Think of it as a lens. Without it, your power might be a diffuse light, less likely to attract attention from afar. With it, that light is focused, concentrated, making it a more potent signal. This is why control is paramount, Elara. An uncontrolled surge of power, amplified by the locket, could be a catastrophic beacon. A controlled manifestation, however, can be directed, perhaps even used as a lure or a misdirection."

He stopped and turned to face her, his expression serious. "The true mastery of your abilities will come not just from learning to unleash your power, but from learning when and how to conceal it. The locket, paradoxically, can aid in this. By learning to control the flow of energy through it, you learn to modulate its outward signal. You learn to whisper your power, rather than shout it."

They continued their trek, the sounds of the forest no longer solely a source of anxiety. Elara found herself consciously reaching for the locket, not with her hands, but with her mind, feeling its steady pulse, its quiet hum of power. She tried to recall the feeling of the controlled energy, the steady current that had emanated from her. It was a fragile sensation, easily disrupted by the exhaustion and the ever-present awareness of their surroundings, but it was there. A nascent skill, a seed of control planted by the locket and nurtured by Kael's guidance.

"Your lineage is tied to the elemental forces, you said?" Elara asked, her mind racing with questions. The concept of elemental magic, once confined to the pages of ancient scrolls in the Academy's forbidden section, was now a tangible reality, woven into the very fabric of her being.

"Indeed," Kael replied. "The bloodline from which you hail has long been associated with the primal forces of earth, air, fire, and water. But it is not a simple manipulation of these elements. It is a deeper connection, a resonance with the very life force that binds them. Your magic is not just about conjuring flames; it is about understanding the nature of heat, about the raw energy that fuels creation and destruction. It is about feeling the earth's deep pulse, the wind's restless spirit, the water's ceaseless flow."

He gestured to a gnarled, ancient oak tree beside the path. "Consider this tree. Its roots draw sustenance from the earth, its leaves breathe the air, its wood has been shaped by the sun's warmth and the rain's embrace. Your magic, at its core, is the ability to commune with and influence these fundamental aspects of existence. The locket acts as a translator, a bridge, helping you to interpret and interact with these forces."

As he spoke, Elara found herself instinctively focusing on the oak tree, her hand resting on the locket. She tried to feel its energy, its ancient stillness, its silent strength. She imagined the locket's glow, not as a defensive shield this time, but as a probe, extending outwards, seeking to understand the tree's essence. She felt a faint thrum, a subtle vibration that seemed to answer her unspoken inquiry. It was not the explosive surge of power from before, but a whisper, a communion.

"I... I think I felt something," she admitted, a note of surprise in her voice. "A deep... rootedness. Like the tree was breathing, but very, very slowly."

Kael's eyes widened slightly, a flicker of genuine astonishment in their depths. "Remarkable. For a first attempt, to feel such a subtle connection... your lineage is strong within you, Elara. The locket has indeed helped you to focus your intent, to bridge the gap between your own nascent power and the elemental forces around you."

He continued to explain, his words painting vivid pictures in Elara's mind. He spoke of how different emotional states could influence the manifestation of her magic, how fear could lead to explosive, uncontrolled bursts, while calm focus could allow for precise, deliberate manipulation. He detailed how the locket could serve as a mental anchor, a point of stability when her emotions threatened to overwhelm her.

"When you feel fear begin to coil in your gut," Kael advised, his voice low and steady, "do not fight it directly. Acknowledge it. Then, immediately, bring your focus to the locket. Feel its warmth, its solid presence. Imagine the fear's energy being drawn into the locket, where it can be tempered, diluted, and rendered harmless. The locket can absorb and transmute negative emotional energy, preventing it from corrupting your magic."

This revelation struck Elara deeply. The memory of the overwhelming fear she had felt against the Gloom Hounds, the sheer panic that had fueled her uncontrolled outburst, was still sharp. To think that the locket could be a buffer, a shield against her own emotional turmoil, was a profound relief. It meant that perhaps she wouldn't always be at the mercy of her own fear.

"So, the locket isn't just about amplifying my power," she mused, her fingers tracing the glowing symbols again, "it's about protecting me from my own reactions too?"

"Precisely," Kael confirmed. "It is a multifaceted artifact, designed to support and guide its wearer. It is a reminder that true power lies not in raw force, but in control, in understanding, and in balance. The more you learn to attune yourself to its resonance, the more you will unlock its capabilities, and the more secure you will become in your own abilities."

He then shifted their focus to the practice of drawing energy. "Imagine your breath," he instructed, "as a continuous flow. As you inhale, draw in the ambient energy of the world around you – the life force of the trees, the subtle hum of the earth, the very essence of the Crimson Moon's light. As you exhale, channel that drawn energy, refined and focused, through the locket."

Elara tried to follow his instructions, her breath deepening, her focus sharpening. It was a complex exercise, requiring a delicate balance of awareness and intent. She imagined the world around her as a tapestry of interwoven energies, and her breath as a tool to pluck threads from that tapestry. She visualized these threads, shimmering and ethereal, flowing into her, and then being gathered and focused by the locket.

For a long moment, nothing seemed to happen. The exhaustion still weighed heavily on her, and the sheer mental effort was draining. Then, a faint warmth, distinct from the locket's own glow, began to spread through her fingertips. It was a subtle sensation, a tingling that felt like the gentle touch of summer rain. She focused, visualizing this warmth gathering at the locket, and as she exhaled, she felt a faint, almost imperceptible pulse of energy radiate outwards.

"There!" Kael exclaimed softly, his eyes bright with satisfaction. "You are beginning to draw upon the ambient energies. This is a crucial step, Elara. It means you are learning to work *with* the world, not just against it. Your magic will become more potent, more sustainable, when you can draw upon the vast reservoirs of power that surround us."

He continued to guide her, his instructions becoming more intricate. He spoke of the importance of intent, of visualizing the desired outcome with absolute clarity. He stressed that a fuzzy, unfocused intent would lead to a muddy, unreliable manifestation of power. He used analogies of a sculptor shaping clay, or an archer aiming at a distant target, emphasizing the precision required.

"Think of the locket as your canvas," he said. "Your intent is the brushstroke. Your magic is the paint. The more precisely you visualize the image you wish to create, the more expertly you wield the brush, the more beautiful and potent your creation will be."

Hours passed under the spectral glow of the Crimson Moon. Elara, though weary, felt a spark of exhilaration. The locket had transformed from a mere memento into a vital tool, an instructor, a partner. She was learning to feel its pulse, to draw strength and clarity from it, to make it an extension of her own will. The wild torrent of power that had erupted from her earlier was still a potent memory, a testament to the raw force she possessed. But now, with the locket as her focal point, she was beginning to glimpse the possibility of control, of direction, of a future where her power was not a source of terror, but a force for good, guided by her own conscious intent. The journey was far from over, the path to mastery long and arduous, but the locket's steady resonance was a constant, reassuring hum, a promise of the power that lay dormant, waiting to be awakened and guided.

The Crimson Moon, a celestial ruby bleeding light across the ink-black sky, cast long, dancing shadows through the ancient boughs of the Whispering Woods. Elara, guided by Kael's steady presence, found herself drawn to a secluded glade. The air here was different, thick with an unseen energy that hummed against her skin, a subtle resonance that mirrored the pulse of the locket nestled against her chest. Kael had instructed her to meditate, to reach inward and explore the burgeoning magic within, using the locket as her anchor.

She sat on a moss-covered stone, the cool, damp earth seeping through her worn tunic. Closing her eyes, she focused on her breath, drawing the mystical energy of the moonlit forest into her lungs. She recalled Kael's words: *"Your breath is a continuous flow. As you inhale, draw in the ambient energy of the world around you – the life force of the trees, the subtle hum of the earth, the very essence of the Crimson Moon's light."* She felt the locket's warmth, a beacon of familiar comfort in the deepening twilight. She imagined the energy she inhaled, a shimmering, ethereal mist, flowing into her and then, with each exhale, being gathered and refined by the locket.

At first, the familiar sensations returned – the faint thrumming of her own awakening magic, the gentle pulse of the artifact. But as she deepened her focus, as she pushed past the exhaustion and the lingering anxieties, something else began to stir. It was like a dream, nascent and fleeting, brushing against the edges of her consciousness. Then, the veil began to thin.

Images, sharp and vivid, flashed behind her eyelids. They were not memories, not in the way she understood them. They were glimpses, fragments of a reality utterly alien, yet strangely familiar. She saw structures of impossible grace, crystalline towers that pierced a sky painted in hues of amethyst and rose. They shimmered with an inner light, seemingly crafted from solidified starlight. Rivers of pure, molten gold flowed between them, not hot and destructive, but radiant and soothing. She saw beings of pure luminescence, their forms fluid and ever-shifting, their movements like the dance of fireflies. They communicated not through spoken words, but through melodies of light and color, weaving intricate patterns in the air that Elara felt more than understood.

These visions were not static. They were alive, imbued with a sense of vibrant, ancient power. She witnessed rituals, breathtaking in their scope and complexity. Figures, robed in garments woven from moonlight and shadow, moved in precise, synchronized patterns around colossal, pulsating crystals. They raised their hands, and the very air seemed to crackle, drawing energy from the stars, from the very fabric of existence, and shaping it into forms of pure magic. The air thrummed with a celestial chorus, a symphony of creation and transformation that resonated deep within her bones.

There were moments of stark beauty, like the sight of a celestial garden where flowers bloomed with petals of pure energy, their scents not olfactory, but emotional – waves of joy, tranquility, and profound wonder washing over her. Then, just as suddenly, the visions would fracture. A fleeting glimpse of an ancient battlefield, the sky rent by beams of raw power, followed by an image of a solitary figure, cloaked and hooded, performing a ritual of immense solemnity before a colossal, obsidian altar. The stark contrast between the vibrant beauty and the shadowed solemnity was jarring, a testament to the complexity of this hidden world.

She saw symbols, intricate and arcane, etched into the very foundations of these shimmering cities, glowing with an inner fire. They were unlike anything she had encountered in her studies, imbued with a power that spoke of ages long past, of forces that shaped reality itself. These symbols seemed to resonate with the carvings on her locket, a silent, echoing communion across the chasm of dimensions.

The intensity of the visions was overwhelming. It was as if a dam had broken within her, unleashing a flood of ancestral echoes, a torrent of knowledge and experience that was not her own, yet felt intrinsically part of her. The raw magic she had awakened within herself, amplified by the locket and fueled by the Crimson Moon's potent light, was acting as a key, unlocking doors to a past so profound, so steeped in magic, that it defied comprehension.

"Elara!" Kael's voice, a grounding force, cut through the swirling kaleidoscope of her inner sight. She gasped, her eyes flying open, the visions dissolving like mist in the morning sun. The glade, the familiar trees, Kael's concerned gaze – they snapped back into sharp focus, but the echo of the hidden world lingered, a vibrant afterimage behind her eyes.

She was trembling, her heart pounding a frantic rhythm against her ribs. The locket was burning hot against her skin, its light pulsing with an accelerated beat, mirroring her own disquiet. "I... I saw things," she stammered, her voice hoarse with disbelief and awe. "A different world... cities of light, beings of... energy. It was so real, Kael. So... ancient."

Kael knelt beside her, his expression a mixture of understanding and concern. He placed a gentle hand on her arm, his touch firm and reassuring. "The echoes," he murmured, his gaze distant, as if he too could sense the residue of the visions. "As your power grows, Elara, as your connection to your lineage deepens, these ancestral memories begin to surface. They are not mere dreams. They are glimpses into the realm your ancestors inhabited, the magical world from which they hailed."

He looked at her, his eyes reflecting the moon's eerie glow. "Your lineage is not of this world, Elara. Not entirely. They were beings of immense magical prowess, deeply connected to the primal forces of creation. The visions you experienced are fragments of that heritage, surfacing as your own abilities awaken. Think of it as a river, Elara. Your magic is the current, and these visions are glimpses of the source, the vast, ancestral ocean from which it flows."

"But... why now?" she whispered, still struggling to process the magnitude of what she had seen. "And why are they so fragmented? So... chaotic?"

"The awakening of such power is rarely a neat or orderly process," Kael explained, his voice patient. "It is like a seed breaking through hardened earth. There is an immense force involved, and the process can be disruptive. Your magic has been stirred by recent events, and the locket, as we discussed, is amplifying and stabilizing this surge. This, in turn, is loosening the gates of your ancestral memory. The visions are chaotic because they are drawn from eons of existence, from a reality vastly different from our own. They are not meant to be a clear narrative, but rather impressions, feelings, potent flashes of truth."

He gestured towards the locket. "The artifact is not just an amplifier and a stabilizer. It is also a conduit to your lineage. It resonates with the very essence of your ancestors, helping to bridge the gap between your present self and their ancient power. It is guiding you, slowly, tentatively, revealing the immensity of what you are becoming."

Elara clutched the locket, its warmth a steady counterpoint to the lingering exhilaration and fear that coursed through her. The visions, though disorienting, had also filled her with a strange sense of purpose, a nascent understanding of the grand tapestry she was now a part of. "It felt... overwhelming," she admitted. "Like I was seeing too much, too fast. And some of it... It was beautiful, but there was a darkness too. A sense of... immense struggle."

"Indeed," Kael agreed, his brow furrowed. "The realm of your ancestors was not a place of perpetual peace. It was a realm where magic flowed like water, where the forces of creation and destruction were in constant flux. Your lineage wielded immense power, but they also faced profound challenges, cosmic battles fought on planes beyond mortal comprehension. The visions are not just showing you the beauty of your heritage, but also the weight of its history, the responsibilities that come with such power."

He met her gaze, his eyes serious. "These visions are both a gift and a burden, Elara. They offer you invaluable insight into your true nature, into the immense potential that lies dormant within you. They are a map, however fragmented, to the world your parents belonged to, a world you are now inextricably linked to. But they also reveal the vastness of what you do not yet know, the immense challenges that lie ahead in understanding and mastering this inherited power."

He rose, offering a hand to help her to her feet. The moonlit glade seemed to shimmer with a new significance, imbued with the spectral echoes of her visions. "The path to understanding your lineage, and to mastering your own abilities, will be long and arduous," Kael stated. "These visions will become more frequent, more vivid, as you grow stronger. You must learn to navigate them, to glean wisdom from their chaos, and to remain grounded in your present reality. They are a reminder of who you are, and who you have the potential to become. But they are not the entirety of your being. You are Elara, the girl from the village, now awakening to a power that transcends worlds."

Elara nodded, her mind still reeling. The visions were a tantalizing glimpse into a world of magic and wonder, a world that felt both impossibly distant and intimately connected to her soul. She saw cities of impossible design, beings of pure energy, and rituals of breathtaking power. It was a world where magic was not a force to be manipulated, but an intrinsic part of existence, woven into the very fabric of reality. The locket, the conduit to this hidden realm, pulsed against her skin, a constant reminder of the legacy she carried.

"It's... so much," she breathed, her voice barely above a whisper. "All of that power, all of that knowledge... It's a part of me?"

"It is," Kael confirmed, his voice resonating with a quiet conviction. "Your lineage was deeply entwined with the very essence of magic. They did not simply wield it; they embodied it. The visions you are experiencing are echoes of that embodiment, surfacing as your own power ignites. Think of them as scattered pages from an ancient tome, each one revealing a facet of your ancestral legacy. The cities of light, the beings of luminescence – these are remnants of a civilization built on pure magical energy, a testament to the heights of power your ancestors achieved."

He paused, letting the weight of his words sink in. "The rituals you witnessed are not mere spectacles. They were the methods by which your ancestors shaped reality, drew upon cosmic energies, and maintained the delicate balance of their world. And the symbols... those are the keys, the foundational glyphs of their magic, imbued with immense power. They are the language of your heritage, a language you are only just beginning to decipher."

Elara's hand instinctively went to the locket, tracing the familiar, yet now profoundly significant, carvings. She could almost feel the ancient power thrumming beneath her fingertips, a silent promise of the secrets it held. "And the darkness I saw?" she asked, her voice tinged with apprehension. "The struggles?"

"Magic, in its rawest form, is neither good nor evil," Kael explained, his gaze steady. "It is a force, a fundamental aspect of existence. Your ancestors, in their pursuit of ultimate power and understanding, certainly encountered opposition. There were forces that sought to corrupt or extinguish their light, and there were internal struggles, the inherent challenges of wielding such immense power responsibly. The visions reflect this duality – the breathtaking beauty of creation and the stark reality of conflict. It is a reminder that great power often comes with great responsibility, and that even the most luminous of paths can be fraught with peril."

He continued, his voice taking on a more measured tone. "The locket, as I've said, acts as a bridge. It allows you to perceive these echoes, to connect with the reservoir of your ancestral memories. But it also serves a vital purpose in helping you to integrate this knowledge without being consumed by it. The fragmentation you experience is, in a way, a protective mechanism. It prevents you from being overwhelmed by the sheer magnitude of what your lineage represents. As you grow in strength and control, these fragments will begin to coalesce, forming a more coherent understanding of your heritage."

Elara looked up at the Crimson Moon, its ethereal glow bathing the forest in an otherworldly light. It seemed to pulse in time with the locket, a celestial symphony that resonated with the awakening magic within her. "So, these visions… they are my inheritance?"

"Precisely," Kael confirmed. "They are the whispers of your blood, the echoes of your past, manifesting as your own power awakens. It is a profound revelation, Elara, and one that will shape your journey. You are not merely a girl who has stumbled upon magic. You are a descendant of beings who commanded it, who shaped worlds with it. This hidden world you glimpse is your legacy, and understanding it is key to understanding yourself."

He walked with her as they continued their journey, the path ahead illuminated by the moon's spectral glow. "The challenges will be many," he continued, his voice a low rumble that carried through the silent woods. "Not only in mastering your own burgeoning abilities, but in understanding the true nature of your heritage. This hidden world, though filled with wonder, is also a place of ancient power, and not all of that power may be benevolent. Your visions will serve as a guide, but also as a warning. They will show you the heights of what is possible, but also the depths of what can be lost."

Elara's hand tightened around the locket. The visions had been overwhelming, disorienting, but they had also ignited a spark within her, a sense of destiny that was both exhilarating and terrifying. She had caught a glimpse of a world beyond her wildest imagination, a world of magic and mystery that was inextricably linked to her own existence. And with each pulse of the locket, with each fragment of ancestral memory that surfaced, she knew that her journey had only just begun. The path ahead was veiled in shadows and illuminated by starlight, a reflection of the hidden world she had glimpsed, and the power that now pulsed within her, waiting to be understood, to be embraced, and ultimately, to be mastered. The weight of her lineage settled upon her, not as a burden, but as a profound calling, a silent promise whispered from the depths of ages past. The visions were more than just echoes; they were a glimpse of the truest self, waiting to be awakened.

CHAPTER 3:

THE PATH OF RUNES

The air changed as they emerged from the dense canopy of the Whispering Woods. Gone was the primal hush of ancient trees, replaced by a cacophony of sounds that assaulted Elara's senses: the rumble of cartwheels on cobblestones, the sharp cries of street vendors hawking their wares, the distant clang of a blacksmith's hammer, and a low, persistent hum that seemed to vibrate from the very stones beneath their feet. Kael had spoken of a city, a bastion of civilization and a nexus of arcane currents, but nothing could have prepared Elara for the sheer, overwhelming spectacle of Aethelgard.

It wasn't merely a collection of buildings; it was a living entity, breathing with a thousand different rhythms. Towering structures of weathered stone, etched with carvings that spoke of a forgotten age, stood shoulder-to-shoulder with more recent constructions of timber and plaster. Yet, even the newer buildings seemed to possess an undercurrent of something more. A subtle shimmer, a fleeting illusion, or perhaps a ward woven into the very mortar, betrayed the fact that magic, in Aethelgard, was not merely an academic pursuit, but an integrated, albeit often subtle, part of daily life.

The sheer density of people was staggering. They flowed through the streets like a multi-hued river, a tapestry of farmers in roughspun tunics, artisans with stained hands, merchants in finer silks, and even a few cloaked figures whose gazes seemed to hold a deeper, more knowing light. Elara, accustomed to the quiet solitude of the orphanage and the hushed reverence of the woods, felt an almost paralyzing sense of being both lost and intensely observed. Every face, every glance, felt like a potential question, a hidden judgment. The locket against her chest pulsed, a gentle, reassuring warmth, as if sensing her unease.

"Aethelgard is… a lot," Kael said, his voice a low murmur beside her, as if he could read her thoughts. "It is where the mundane and the magical meet, often with a rough embrace. The city thrives on the flow of goods and information, but also on the ebb and flow of arcane energies. Many who possess even a flicker of talent, or a thirst for forbidden knowledge, find their way here eventually."

He guided her through a throng of people, his presence a steady anchor in the swirling chaos. "We need to be discreet, Elara. Your awakening is recent, and as you've seen, your lineage carries a certain… weight. Not everyone in Aethelgard is friendly to those who tread the path of runes, especially if they are perceived as a threat, or worse, a potential source of power to be exploited."

They entered a wide plaza, a vibrant heart beating at the city's core. Here, the sensory overload intensified. Stalls overflowed with exotic spices that scented the air with an intoxicating mix of the familiar and the alien. Bolts of shimmering fabric, woven with threads that seemed to catch the light with an unnatural brilliance, were draped alongside sturdy leather goods. A gnome, no taller than Elara's waist, haggled animatedly over a basket of luminous fungi, his voice a high-pitched squeak that somehow carried over the din. Across from him, a towering woman with skin the color of polished ebony demonstrated a self-stirring cauldron, a faint blue aura shimmering around its rim.

Elara found herself drawn to the architecture. Much of it was ancient, the stone worn smooth by centuries of wind and rain, carved with intricate knotwork and stylized beasts that seemed to stare with vacant, knowing eyes. Yet, interspersed with these monolithic structures were newer buildings, their timber frames displaying a curious resilience, their windows seeming to refract light in peculiar ways. She saw a baker's shop, its oven emitting a faint warmth that felt inexplicably soothing, and a stall selling dried herbs, where the plants themselves seemed to emit a soft, internal glow.

"The city was built upon a convergence of ley lines," Kael explained, his eyes scanning the periphery, ever watchful. "The founders, long before the age of kings and empires, understood the power inherent in this location. They harnessed it, channeled it, and wove it into the very fabric of Aethelgard. That's why you feel that hum, that underlying energy. It's the lifeblood of the city, a constant, subtle magic."

He led her away from the main plaza, down a narrower street lined with shops displaying arcane curiosities. Potions in vials of every conceivable color bubbled gently on shelves. Books bound in strange leathers, their pages whispering of forgotten lore, were stacked precariously high. A merchant with a scarred face and eyes like chips of obsidian eyed them as they passed, a calculating glint in his gaze. Elara felt a prickle of unease. This was a place of commerce, yes, but also a place where secrets were bought and sold, and where knowledge was a currency more valuable than gold.

"We need to find the Argent Archive," Kael stated, his voice firm. "It is one of the few places in Aethelgard where one can find true scholarly resources, and more importantly, information on the runes you saw in your visions. It is also, thankfully, a place that values discretion above all else."

As they navigated the labyrinthine streets, Elara couldn't help but notice the subtle discrepancies, the almost imperceptible magical undercurrents that rippled beneath the surface of the mundane. A stray cat, its fur the color of twilight, darted across their path, and for a fleeting moment, its eyes glowed with an unnatural sapphire light. A flowerbox on a windowsill, filled with ordinary-looking blossoms, pulsed with a faint, rhythmic luminescence. These were not grand displays of power, but rather small, intimate enchantments, woven into the everyday fabric of the city, visible only to those who knew how to look.

They passed by a guard post, two burly men in city livery standing with their spears held loosely. Yet, as Elara glanced at their armor, she saw faint, silver runes etched into the metal, pulsing with a soft, protective light. These were not mere decorations; they were wards, imbued with specific enchantments to repel harm. Even the city's defenses were woven with magic.

"The city guard are not all warriors in the traditional sense," Kael murmured, as if sensing her observation. "Many of them are trained in basic warding and scrying. They can sense disturbances, detect hostile intent. It's a necessary precaution in a city like this, where threats can come in many forms, both seen and unseen."

He paused, gesturing towards a narrow alleyway that opened up into a small, secluded courtyard. The sounds of the bustling city were muted here, replaced by the gentle trickle of a fountain and the rustling of leaves from a gnarled, ancient tree that dominated the space. The air here was cooler, cleaner, imbued with a sense of calm that was a welcome respite.

"This is a safe haven," Kael said, his voice softening slightly. "A place to gather ourselves before we venture deeper into the heart of Aethelgard. Your visions, Elara, are a powerful gift, but they are also a glimpse into a world that is far more complex and dangerous than you can currently comprehend. Aethelgard is a crossroads, a place where such complexities are amplified. Here, you will encounter not only the knowledge you seek, but also those who would exploit your burgeoning power."

He met her gaze, his eyes serious. "You must learn to discern. To see beyond the surface. To understand that not all enchantments are benevolent, and not all individuals who offer knowledge are true allies. The orphanage provided you with a foundation of survival, but here, you must build upon that with wisdom and a keen sense of awareness."

Elara nodded, her mind racing. The visions had been overwhelming, yes, but they had also sparked a profound curiosity. The city, with its blend of the ancient and the arcane, felt like a tangible

70

manifestation of the world she had glimpsed in her meditations. It was a world where magic was not a fairy tale, but a force that shaped lives, built cities, and influenced the very air one breathed.

"You mentioned the path of runes," Elara said, her voice gaining a steadier tone. "The symbols I saw... they were runes, weren't they?"

"Indeed," Kael confirmed. "They are the foundational language of much of the magic that exists, or at least, that existed in its purest form. Your ancestors, as you've begun to understand, were masters of this art. The visions were not random flashes; they were glimpses of your heritage, etched into the fabric of your being, waiting to be reawakened. The runes are the keys, the keys to unlocking that power, to understanding the forces that shaped your lineage, and ultimately, to understanding yourself."

He picked up a smooth, grey stone from the edge of the fountain, turning it over in his fingers. "Every symbol, every glyph, carries a specific resonance, a particular function. They can channel energy, create barriers, influence minds, and even alter the very nature of reality. Your ancestors didn't just wield magic; they understood its underlying structure, its fundamental language."

He then gestured to the intricate carvings on the ancient stone walls surrounding the courtyard. "Look closely, Elara. Do you see the similarities? The patterns? These are not mere decorations. They are a form of script, a rudimentary form of runic inscription that has been passed down, adapted, and woven into the city's very being. The builders of Aethelgard understood the potency of such symbols."

Elara studied the carvings, her eyes tracing the curves and angles. There was a familiar flow to them, a rhythmic quality that echoed the patterns she had seen in her visions. The runes she had witnessed had been more complex, more vibrant, glowing with an inner fire, but the underlying principles, the fundamental shapes, seemed to be

71

present here, muted, perhaps, by time and the mundane influences of the city.

"So, the Argent Archive... they will have information on these runes?" she asked, her voice laced with a newfound hope.

"They will," Kael assured her. "The Archive is a repository of knowledge gathered over centuries, meticulously cataloged and guarded. Scholars, mages, and seekers of truth have contributed to its vast collection. Within its hallowed halls, you may find texts that explain the origins of the runes, their meanings, and their applications. It is a place of learning, Elara, a place where you can begin to bridge the gap between the fragmented visions you experience and a structured understanding of your abilities."

He then looked at her, his gaze piercing. "But remember what I said. The Archive is not a sanctuary from the dangers of Aethelgard. It is a destination, and the journey there will require your constant vigilance. There are many who covet the knowledge held within its walls, and many who would see that knowledge used for darker purposes. You must learn to navigate these currents, to protect yourself, and to choose your allies wisely."

As they stepped out of the secluded courtyard and back into the vibrant chaos of the city streets, Elara felt a subtle shift within her. The initial overwhelm had begun to subside, replaced by a quiet determination. Aethelgard was a city of contrasts, a place of immense potential and hidden peril, a world far removed from the quiet confines of the orphanage. But for the first time, she felt a sense of belonging, not to the city itself, but to the grand, unfolding narrative of her own destiny. The path ahead was uncertain, shrouded in the mysteries of her lineage and the arcane secrets of the runes, but she knew, with a certainty that resonated deep within her soul, that she was finally on the right path. The city of Aethelgard was not just a destination; it was a crucible, where the fragments of her past would be forged into the strength of her future.

Kael led her through a maze of bustling markets, where the air grew thick with the scents of exotic spices, roasting meats, and the strangely sweet perfume of enchanted incense. Merchants shouted their wares, their voices a constant drone that Elara was slowly beginning to filter out. Children chased each other through the throngs, their laughter a bright counterpoint to the more somber murmur of adult conversation. It was a city alive with the mundane, a place where people went about their daily lives, largely oblivious to the deeper currents of magic that flowed beneath the surface.

"The Argent Archive is located in the scholar's district," Kael explained, his voice low. "It's a more subdued area, less frequented by the common folk, more by those who seek knowledge. Be prepared for the atmosphere, Elara. It's not a place of vibrant displays of power, but of hushed whispers, ancient texts, and watchful librarians."

They turned down a street where the buildings grew taller, their facades more austere. The stone here was darker, more polished, and the intricate carvings that adorned the older structures were more purposeful, less ornamental. There was a sense of gravitas here, a palpable feeling of accumulated knowledge. The hum of latent energy was still present, but it was more refined, more controlled, like a powerful engine purring quietly beneath a polished hood.

Elara noticed small, discreet symbols etched above doorways – symbols that Kael identified as wards of protection and concealment. These were not the bold, declarative runes of power that she had glimpsed in her visions, but subtler inscriptions, designed to safeguard knowledge and keep prying eyes at bay. Even here, in this sanctuary of learning, magic was an essential, albeit understated, element.

Finally, they arrived at a grand, imposing structure that seemed to absorb the surrounding light. Its facade was of smooth, dark obsidian, inlaid with veins of what appeared to be pure, solidified moonlight. The entrance was a single, massive archway, flanked by silent, imposing statues of robed figures, their faces obscured by deep hoods. No merchants hawked their wares here, no boisterous crowds filled the square. Instead, there was a quiet reverence, an atmosphere of deep contemplation.

"This is it," Kael said, his voice a hushed tone. "The Argent Archive. Within these walls lies a wealth of knowledge that could take a lifetime to decipher. But remember, Elara, the true understanding of your heritage will not come solely from dusty tomes. It will come from integrating that knowledge, from connecting it with the power that is already stirring within you. The Archive is a guide, not a destination."

As they approached the entrance, a figure emerged from the shadows of the archway. He was an old man, his frame stooped, his face a roadmap of wrinkles. He wore a simple, dark robe, and his eyes, though clouded with age, held a sharpness that belied his physical appearance. He carried a gnarled staff, its surface smooth from years of handling.

"Travelers," the old man said, his voice a dry rustle, like leaves skittering across stone. "The Argent Archive does not welcome the merely curious. What is it you seek within its hallowed halls?"

Kael stepped forward, his expression respectful. "We seek knowledge, elder. Knowledge of the ancient runes and of the lineage they represent. My companion, Elara, has recently awakened to a profound heritage, and we believe the answers we seek may be found within your collection."

The old man's gaze settled upon Elara, his eyes seeming to bore into her very soul. Elara felt a familiar tingle, a subtle resonance that mirrored the locket's warmth. He looked at her for a long moment, his expression unreadable, before turning his attention back to Kael.

"A heritage, you say?" the old man mused, stroking his chin. "The path of runes is a dangerous one, often trodden by those who are unprepared for its burdens. The Archive can offer guidance, but it cannot shield you from the consequences of your choices, nor from the attention you may draw."

He then looked at Elara again, a flicker of something akin to recognition in his ancient eyes. "The locket you wear... it resonates with the old ways. A potent artifact, indeed. Very well. You may enter. But be warned: the Archive demands respect, and its knowledge must be earned. I am Librarian Theron, and I will be your guide within these walls."

With a nod, Theron turned and led them into the Archive. The interior was vast and silent, the air cool and still, carrying the faint, comforting scent of aged parchment and dried ink. Towering shelves, stretching higher than Elara could see, lined the walls, filled with countless volumes, scrolls, and ancient artifacts. Light filtered in from high, narrow windows, casting long, spectral beams across the hushed space.

"This place is a testament to centuries of learning," Theron said, his voice echoing softly in the cavernous hall. "Knowledge from across the realms, gathered and preserved. Here, you will find histories, treatises on magic, astronomical charts, and, of course, texts pertaining to the runes. But be warned, child," he addressed Elara directly, his gaze intense, "the runes are not mere symbols to be memorized. They are the very building blocks of existence, imbued with power that can shape reality itself. To wield them without understanding is to invite chaos."

He led them through labyrinthine corridors, each turn revealing more shelves, more books, more quiet corners where scholars, hunched over ancient texts, seemed lost to the world. Elara felt a thrill of awe and trepidation. This was it, the place where she could begin to unravel the mystery of her visions, to understand the power that was awakening within her.

"Your visions of cities of light, of beings of luminescence," Theron continued, as if sensing her thoughts. "These are not mere fantasies, child. They are echoes of a time when magic flowed more freely, when beings of immense power walked the earth, or perhaps, realms beyond. The runes were their language, their tool, their very essence."

He stopped before a particularly large section of shelves, laden with ancient, leather-bound tomes. The air around them seemed to shimmer with a latent energy, a faint, almost imperceptible hum. "Here," Theron announced, his voice resonating with importance. "This is where your journey into the runes truly begins. These volumes contain ancient lore, recovered from forgotten civilizations, detailing the fundamental runic alphabets, their associated energies, and their applications."

He gestured to a specific book, its cover embossed with a complex, swirling pattern that seemed to shift and reform as Elara watched. "This, for instance, is the 'Codex Lumina'. It speaks of the runes of light, the very glyphs that formed the foundations of your ancestors' magnificent cities. It details how they were used to channel celestial energies, to create structures of impossible beauty, and to communicate across vast distances."

He then pointed to another, darker volume, bound in what looked like dragon hide. "And this, the 'Grimoire Umbra', details the runes of shadow, of manipulation, of power that can be both formidable and dangerous. Understanding the duality of such forces is crucial, child. For every rune of creation, there is often a corresponding rune of destruction, a reflection of the balance that governs all things."

Theron then turned his attention to Elara. "Your locket is a key, child. It resonates with the frequencies of these runes, and it will help you to decipher them, to feel their power. But the ultimate mastery will come from within you. You must learn to feel the energy, to shape it, to guide it with your will. The visions have shown you glimpses, but the Archive will provide the map. The journey from map to mastery, however, is yours alone to forge."

As Theron began to explain the fundamental principles of runic inscription, Elara felt a profound sense of wonder. The symbols, once abstract and fleeting in her visions, began to take on form and meaning. She learned of the foundational runes, the primal energies they represented, and how they could be combined and manipulated to create more complex enchantments. It was a language unlike any she had ever encountered, a language that spoke not just to the mind, but to the very soul.

The whispers of ancient magic in Aethelgard were no longer just background noise; they were becoming a conversation, a dialogue that Elara was finally beginning to understand. The path of runes, though arduous, was unfolding before her, and in the hallowed halls of the Argent Archive, she felt the first stirrings of true comprehension, the nascent dawn of a power she was only just beginning to grasp. The city, with its blend of the mundane and the magical, was proving to be the perfect, if challenging, cradle for her awakening.

The hushed reverence of the Argent Archive began to feel like a stifling cloak after days of relentless study. Elara had absorbed countless pages of lore, her mind a swirling vortex of ancient scripts and forgotten incantations. Librarian Theron, a patient guide through the labyrinthine shelves, had provided them with texts that spoke of the fundamental energies underpinning runic magic, the primal forces of creation, decay, stasis, and flux. She'd learned of the elemental runes, the glyphs that resonated with fire, water, earth, and air, and how these could be woven into spells of immense power. Yet, despite the wealth of information, a crucial piece remained missing. The locket, a constant, warm presence against her skin, still held its deepest secrets, its intricate symbols a tantalizing puzzle that the Archive's vast collection had only partially illuminated. The texts hinted at a more profound, personal connection to these glyphs, a lineage-bound magic that transcended mere academic understanding.

"The Archive is a treasury of knowledge, Elara," Kael said one evening, as they sat in their quiet rented rooms, the city's hum a distant lullaby. He gestured to the stack of scrolls beside her. "But sometimes, the most potent truths are not found in books, but in the hands of those who have lived them."

Elara looked up, her eyes tired but alight with a nascent fire. "You mean... someone who still practices the old ways? Someone who understands the locket?"

Kael nodded, his gaze thoughtful. "The texts speak of rune-carvers, artisans who imbue objects with magic, shaping raw energy into tangible forms. They are keepers of ancient traditions, often living apart from the bustling cities, dedicating their lives to the craft. If anyone can help us understand the locket's deeper significance and your connection to it, it would be such a master."

Their search for this elusive master began subtly, a series of hushed inquiries in the city's more discreet circles. They spoke with seasoned merchants who traded in arcane artifacts, with scholars whose interests strayed beyond the sanctioned texts of the Archive, and even with a few less-than-savory individuals who dealt in forbidden knowledge. The name that recurred, whispered with a mixture of awe and caution, was that of Master Borin. He was said to be ancient, a recluse who lived in the shadowed outskirts of Aethelgard, his workshop a place steeped in centuries of runic mastery. Few had seen him in decades, fewer still had been granted audience, but all agreed on one thing: his skill with runes was unparalleled, a living link to the magic of ages past.

Navigating the labyrinthine alleys that led away from the scholar's district was a descent into a different Aethelgard. The polished obsidian and the hushed reverence of the Argent Archive gave way to rough-hewn stone, shadowed alcoves, and the lingering scent of woodsmoke and something metallic, something that hinted at forge fires. The city's hum here was different, less a vibrant pulse and more a low, resonant thrum, as if the very earth beneath their feet held a deep, ancient secret. They passed by abandoned workshops, their windows dark and forlorn, and saw the occasional furtive figure slip into a shadowed doorway, their purpose as opaque as the encroaching twilight.

"Borin's domain is... particular," Kael murmured, his senses on high alert. "He guards his solitude fiercely. We must approach with respect, Elara. He is not one to suffer fools, or those who come with ill intent."

The address they had been given led them to a part of the city that felt like a forgotten limb, overgrown and neglected. Twisted vines clung to crumbling walls, and the air grew heavy with the scent of damp earth and blooming nightshade. They found themselves before a structure that seemed less built and more grown, its stone walls weathered and ancient, adorned with moss and creeping ivy. It was a place that seemed to exhale the passage of time. Above the heavy, iron-bound door, etched into the stone with a precision that defied its apparent age, was a single, complex rune – a symbol that resonated with a deep, grounding energy, a ward of profound protection.

Kael knocked, the sound echoing unnervingly in the stillness. For a long moment, there was only silence. Then, with a deep, groaning creak, the massive door swung inward, revealing not a welcoming entryway, but a dimly lit expanse that smelled of metal, stone dust, and a potent, indefinable arcane energy. The air within seemed to vibrate, a palpable field of power that made the hairs on Elara's arms stand on end. This was no mere workshop; it was a sanctum.

"Enter," a voice rasped from the gloom, dry and ancient as bone. It seemed to emanate from the shadows themselves. "Do not dawdle."

They stepped inside, and the door swung shut behind them with a heavy thud, plunging them into a world of shadow and flickering light. The space was vast, a cavernous interior filled with an astonishing collection of objects. Shelves, hewn from dark, unvarnished wood, climbed the walls, laden with an eclectic assortment of artifacts. There were weapons of peculiar design – swords with hilts etched with glowing glyphs, axes whose blades seemed to hum with stored force, and bows crafted from materials Elara couldn't identify, their strings shimmering with latent power. Interspersed among these were tools of strange and intricate craftsmanship: hammers that seemed to glow with internal heat, chisels that gleamed with an impossible sharpness, and anvils that bore the scars of millennia of use, each mark a testament to some legendary forging.

Dust motes danced in the shafts of light that pierced the gloom from high, narrow windows, illuminating the sheer volume of accumulated arcane energy. Runes were everywhere. They were carved into the very stones of the floor, inlaid into the metal of the tools, and painted onto the surfaces of ancient scrolls stacked haphazardly on benches. Some glowed with a faint, inner light – soft blues, emerald greens, and molten golds – while others remained dormant, their power waiting to be awakened. The air itself seemed thick with the residue of countless spells, a potent brew of intent and execution.

And then Elara saw him. Seated at a large, worn workbench, bathed in the focused glow of a magical lamp that cast intricate runic patterns onto the surface, was an old man. He was diminutive, his frame stooped with age, but his hands, gnarled and calloused, moved with a surprising deftness. He wore a thick, leather apron stained with countless materials, and his white hair was a wild halo around his head. His face was a tapestry of deep wrinkles, but his eyes, small and bright, glinted with an unnerving sharpness, like chips of obsidian catching the light.

He looked up from the intricate carving he was meticulously etching onto a bronze amulet, his gaze fixing on Elara. There was no surprise in his eyes, no curiosity, only a deep, penetrating assessment that seemed to strip away all pretense. It was a look that spoke of having seen countless souls, each with their own burdens and destinies.

"You are the one," the old man rasped, his voice like stones grinding together. He gestured with a chisel towards Elara. "The one who carries the echo. I felt your approach, like a ripple in the ancient currents."

Kael stepped forward, bowing his head respectfully. "Master Borin, we seek your wisdom. My companion, Elara, has been touched by a lineage of runic magic, a heritage she is only beginning to understand. We were told that your craft and knowledge are without equal."

Borin grunted, a sound that could have been agreement or disdain. He set down his chisel, the rhythmic scraping ceasing, and his eyes narrowed as he turned his full attention to Elara. He didn't speak for a long moment, his gaze lingering on her, then drifting to the locket that rested against her chest.

"The locket," he said, his voice softening infinitesimally. "A relic of the Elder Weavers. It sings a forgotten song." He beckoned with a crooked finger. "Approach, girl. Let this old craftsman see the legacy you carry."

Hesitantly, Elara stepped closer, Kael a reassuring presence at her side. As she stood before the workbench, Borin's sharp eyes scanned her, his gaze moving from her face to the locket, and then, with a surprising intensity, to her hands.

"Your lineage," he mused, more to himself than to them. "It runs deep. The Elder Weavers were the first to understand the language of creation, to weave the primal energies into tangible form. They saw the runes not as symbols, but as living entities, capable of shaping the very fabric of existence." He picked up a small, rough-hewn stone from his bench, its surface unmarked. "Most think of runes as mere etchings. They are this," he tapped the stone, "and yet, so much more. They are conduits, anchors, keys."

He then gestured to the amulet he had been working on, a complex arrangement of interlocking symbols that seemed to pulse with a faint, inner warmth. "This amulet, for instance, is a ward of protection. Carved with runes of strength and resilience, it will deflect minor physical harm and dampen hostile magical intent. Simple, yet effective. But the magic within your locket... that is of a different order entirely."

He reached out a trembling, but surprisingly steady, hand, and Elara instinctively flinched, but Borin's fingers gently brushed against the locket's cool metal. A faint, ethereal glow emanated from the amulet, a soft, silvery light that seemed to respond to his touch.

"See?" Borin said, a flicker of something akin to excitement in his ancient eyes. "It recognizes the resonance of the old ways. The runes on this locket are not merely decorative. They are woven with the very essence of your ancestry, imbued with a power that sleeps, waiting for the right hand to awaken it."

He picked up a different tool, a delicate stylus tipped with what looked like a sliver of crystallized moonlight. "The Archive gave you knowledge of the *how*, the *what*," he continued, his voice gaining strength. "They taught you the theoretical. But I... I will teach you the *why*, and more importantly, the *feel*. The runes are not just shapes on stone or metal. They are vibrations, energies, emotions. To truly master them, you must learn to feel them, to become one with their song."

Borin then began to speak, his words weaving a narrative that painted a vivid picture of a world long past. He spoke of the Elder Weavers, not as mere mages or artisans, but as sculptors of reality, who used the primal runes to raise cities from the earth, to command the elements, and to forge bonds with creatures of pure magic. He described how they didn't just inscribe runes; they *breathed* them into existence, channeling their life force, their will, their very souls into the act of creation.

"Your visions," Borin said, his gaze meeting Elara's directly. "The cities of light, the ethereal beings... these are not mere dreams, child. They are echoes of that time, imprinted upon your spirit. The runes you saw were not just symbols; they were manifestations of the Weaver's power, reflections of the pure energies they commanded."

He pointed to a particularly intricate knotwork design carved into the leg of his workbench. "This, for example, is a rudimentary rune of binding, a simple iteration of the complex glyphs that held their cities together, that linked mind to mind across vast distances. The locket you wear contains a more profound version, a key that can unlock not just specific enchantments, but the very pathways of your lineage's power."

Borin then instructed Elara to place her hand on the locket. "Focus," he commanded gently. "Feel its warmth. Now, let your intention flow into it. Think of the runes you saw in your visions. Don't try to recall their shapes precisely, but rather their *essence*. Their feeling."

Elara closed her eyes, her breath catching in her throat. She focused on the locket, its familiar warmth spreading through her palm. She thought of the luminous cities, the swirling patterns of light, the sense of boundless possibility. At first, there was only the familiar sensation. But then, as Borin's quiet encouragement guided her, a subtle shift occurred. A faint resonance seemed to pulse from the locket, an answering thrum that vibrated within her very bones. She could almost feel the lines of the runes, not as distinct shapes, but as currents of energy, flowing and intertwining.

"Yes," Borin rasped, his voice filled with a quiet triumph. "You feel it. That is the beginning. The runes are a language, but like any language, their deepest meaning is not in the sounds themselves, but in the emotions and intentions they convey."

He then picked up a shard of what looked like obsidian, impossibly smooth and dark. "The Elder Weavers understood the inherent duality of power," he explained, turning the obsidian in his gnarled fingers. "Every rune of creation has its counterpart of entropy, every glyph of light its shadow. This is the balance that governs all things, the constant interplay of forces that shapes the universe."

He placed the obsidian shard on the workbench and then, with his stylus, began to etch a symbol onto its surface. As he worked, the stone itself seemed to absorb the light, a vortex of darkness blooming where the stylus traced its path. Elara watched, mesmerized, as the glyph formed, a sharp, angular rune that seemed to pull at the very light in the room.

"This," Borin declared, holding up the obsidian shard, "is a rune of negation, a symbol that can unravel enchantments, silence magic, and even extinguish life. It is the shadow to the light, the silence to the song." He then picked up a smooth, pale stone, like river-worn quartz. "And this is a rune of illumination, a glyph that amplifies, clarifies, and brings forth hidden truths. It is the light that banishes shadow."

He placed the two stones side-by-side. "The Elder Weavers wielded both. They understood that true power lies not in embracing one extreme, but in understanding and mastering the interplay between them. Your lineage, Elara, carries the legacy of that mastery. Your locket is a testament to that understanding, a key that can unlock both the light and the shadow within you."

Borin then guided Elara through a series of exercises. He had her trace runes in the air with her fingers, focusing on the intention behind each glyph. He had her hold smooth stones and metallic ingots, encouraging her to feel the innate energies within them, to sense the latent runic potential waiting to be awakened. He spoke of the 'soul-etching' process, a method where the carver's own spiritual essence was infused into the runes, making them an extension of their being.

"The Archive teaches you the alphabet," Borin explained, his voice growing raspy with the effort of his prolonged discourse. "I teach you to speak. To feel the rhythm of the words, the weight of their meaning, the consequence of their utterance." He gestured to a vast collection of raw materials: rough slabs of granite, polished oak, sheets of copper and silver, ingots of iron and bronze. "Each material has its own resonance, its own affinity for certain runes. Granite holds the stubborn power of earth; oak embraces the slow, deliberate growth of time; copper conducts the vibrant energies of thought and communication; silver resonates with the subtle magic of the moon and intuition."

He then turned his attention back to the locket. "The symbols on your locket are not simple inscriptions. They are a narrative, a story etched in the very fabric of your lineage. There are runes of lineage, of protection, and, I suspect, of a powerful awakening. To fully decipher them, we must not just understand the runes themselves, but the context in which they were carved, the purpose for which they were imbued."

Borin spent days with Elara, patiently guiding her through the intricacies of runic carving. He showed her how to prepare the surfaces, how to hold the tools, and how to focus her will into the act of inscription. He demonstrated the delicate art of imbuing a rune with specific intent, explaining how a slight shift in pressure, a subtle alteration in the angle of the chisel, could change the rune's very nature. He taught her the runes of warding, of binding, of channeling elemental energies, and of influencing the senses.

One afternoon, as Elara was attempting to carve a simple rune of warmth onto a small wooden disc, her brow furrowed in concentration, Borin watched her with a knowing gaze. Her hands, though still uncertain, were growing steadier. The locket against her chest pulsed with a gentle rhythm, a silent encouragement.

"You are learning to listen to the stone, girl," Borin said, his voice rough but not unkind. "To feel its resistance, its willingness. That is the first step to becoming a true carver. The wood, the stone, the metal – they are not inert. They are vessels, waiting to be filled. Your will, your intention, your very essence, is the energy that fills them."

He picked up a smooth, dark stone. "This stone, for instance, has the resonance of earth, of stability. If you were to carve a rune of protection upon it, it would become a potent amulet, resistant to physical harm. But if you were to imbue it with a rune of passage, it might become a key, allowing you to traverse certain barriers."

Kael, meanwhile, spent his time observing Borin's vast collection, his sharp eyes scanning the shelves and workbenches. He would often ask Borin about specific artifacts, their history, and the runes that adorned them. Borin, in turn, would answer with curt, insightful explanations, revealing fragments of lore that spoke of legendary heroes, forgotten empires, and magical cataclysms. He spoke of the "Rune Lords," an ancient order of master carvers who could shape mountains with their craft, and of the "Whispering Runes," glyphs so potent they could alter the very fabric of time and space.

As Elara's skill grew, Borin began to focus on the locket itself. He would have her hold it, meditate on its symbols, and then attempt to replicate certain aspects of them in her own carvings. He explained that the locket was not just a repository of power, but a map, guiding her towards the deeper truths of her lineage.

"The locket contains fragments of the 'Great Runes, '" Borin revealed one evening, his voice hushed with reverence. "The primal glyphs from which all others are derived. They are the foundations of creation, the very language of the cosmos. Your ancestors, the

Elder Weavers, were masters of these Great Runes. To understand them is to understand the source of all magic."

He indicated a particularly complex symbol on the locket, a swirling pattern that seemed to shift and change as Elara focused on it. "This, for instance, is a manifestation of the 'Rune of Becoming'. It speaks of change, of transformation, of the potential inherent in all things. It is the rune that allows for growth, for evolution, for the very act of creation." He then pointed to another, a sharp, angular glyph that seemed to hum with contained power. "And this... this is a fragment of the 'Rune of Binding'. It speaks of connection, of unity, of the forces that hold existence together."

Borin's sanctum was a place where time seemed to warp and bend. Days blurred into weeks as Elara immersed herself in the arduous but exhilarating process of learning. She learned to feel the distinct energies of each rune, to discern their subtle differences, and to understand their interconnectedness. She felt the grounding power of the earth runes, the fiery passion of the fire runes, the fluid adaptability of the water runes, and the airy freedom of the air runes. She began to see how these primal forces could be combined and woven together, creating complex patterns of magic that were both beautiful and immensely powerful.

Borin, though gruff, proved to be an infinitely patient teacher. He pushed Elara, demanding her full attention and unwavering focus, but he also recognized the spark of innate talent that burned within her. He saw in her not just a student, but a potential successor, a vessel for the ancient knowledge that he himself had guarded for so long.

"The locket," he said to Elara one crisp morning, as they worked with molten silver, attempting to cast a rune of amplification, "is more than an heirloom. It is a key, forged in the fires of your ancestors' will. It holds the resonance of their power, their knowledge, and their spirit. As you learn to understand and control the runes, you will also learn to unlock the deepest secrets held within them."

He explained that the Elder Weavers had not just carved runes onto objects; they had woven them into the very fabric of their beings, inscribing them onto their souls. This, he emphasized, was the ultimate goal: not just to wield magic, but to *become* it. Elara's visions, her innate sensitivity to the arcane, were proof that she was on that path, a path that the locket was designed to illuminate.

"The world outside this sanctum," Borin rasped, his gaze drifting towards the heavy, rune-inscribed door, "is filled with those who crave power, who seek to exploit the ancient ways for their own gain. They understand the *what* of runes, but not the *why*. They can replicate a symbol, but they cannot feel its soul. Your lineage, child, is a bulwark against such corruption. The Elder Weavers were guardians of balance, wielders of both light and shadow, and you... You are their inheritor."

As Elara continued to practice, she began to experience subtle changes. Her senses sharpened, the world around her taking on a new vibrancy. She could feel the subtle magical currents flowing through the city, the almost imperceptible hum of power that permeated everything. She found herself intuitively understanding the language of the runes, their meaning and intent resonating within her on a deeper level. The locket, too, seemed to respond to her growing understanding, its warmth intensifying, its subtle glow becoming more pronounced during her practice sessions.

Borin, observing her progress, finally deemed her ready to delve into the more profound secrets of her lineage. He led her to a hidden alcove within his workshop, a space concealed behind a wall of ancient, rune-etched stone. The air here was different, charged with an ancient, almost overwhelming, energy. In the center of the alcove, resting on a pedestal of dark, unyielding stone, was an object unlike anything Elara had ever seen. It was a sphere, roughly the size of a human head, crafted from a material that seemed to absorb and refract light simultaneously, creating an illusion of impossible depth. Etched into its surface were patterns of such intricate beauty and complexity that Elara's breath caught in her throat. These were not mere runes; they were living tapestries of light and energy, shifting and reforming with a silent, celestial rhythm.

"The Heartstone," Borin whispered, his voice filled with an almost palpable reverence. "A creation of the first Elder Weavers. It holds the collective knowledge, the accumulated wisdom, and the residual power of our lineage. It is the culmination of their understanding of the Great Runes, a testament to their mastery of existence itself."

He gestured for Elara to approach. "This is where the true deciphering of your locket begins. The Heartstone resonates with the same primal energies. It will amplify your connection, revealing the deeper meanings of the symbols you carry, and more importantly, unlocking the dormant power within you." He placed Elara's hand, still clutching the locket, onto the cool, smooth surface of the Heartstone.

As her hand made contact, a wave of pure energy surged through Elara, a torrent of sensation that was both overwhelming and exhilarating. The locket blazed with an intense, silver light, and the runes etched onto the Heartstone seemed to leap to life, swirling and dancing around her. Images flooded her mind – not fragmented visions this time, but clear, coherent visions of the Elder Weavers, their hands moving with grace and power as they carved the very essence of reality. She saw them shaping mountains, commanding stars, and weaving worlds with threads of pure, incandescent magic. The runes on her locket pulsed in sync with the Heartstone, each symbol now revealing its true name, its true purpose, its true power. The Rune of Becoming, the Rune of Binding, and others she had only glimpsed in her most profound visions now stood clear and distinct in her mind's eye. Borin's gruff tutelage, the knowledge from the Argent Archive, and the primal resonance of the Heartstone and her locket converged, forging a connection between her past, present, and future. The path of runes was no longer an abstract concept; it was a tangible, living force, and she was finally beginning to truly walk it.

The air in Borin's sanctum crackled with an energy Elara had only previously felt as a distant hum, a potentiality lurking at the edges of her awareness. Now, it was a palpable force, pressing in on her, urging her to a deeper understanding. The locket, nestled against her skin, felt warmer than usual, a silent echo of the arcane currents swirling around them. Borin, his gnarled fingers moving with the practiced grace of a master craftsman, laid out a series of polished stones before her, each bearing a single, elegantly carved rune.

"These are not merely symbols, Elara," he rasped, his voice a low rumble that seemed to resonate with the very stones beneath their feet. "They are keys. Each one unlocks a particular chamber of knowledge, a specific facet of the primal forces that shape our world." He tapped a rune that depicted a swirling vortex. "This, for instance, is a glyph of Flux. It speaks of change, of movement, of the inherent instability of all things. It is the force that drives creation, but also the hand that brings decay."

He then pointed to a rune shaped like a solid, unyielding mountain. "And this is Stasis. It represents permanence, stillness, the refusal to yield. It is the anchor that holds the cosmos together, but also the force that can lead to stagnation."

Elara traced the Flux rune with her fingertip, a faint warmth emanating from the carved lines. She could feel a subtle thrumming beneath her skin, a resonance that seemed to mirror the concept of ceaseless motion. The locket pulsed in response, as if acknowledging the connection. "So, the runes are not just words, but... concepts made manifest?" she ventured, her voice hushed with awe.

Borin grunted, a sound that conveyed both agreement and the immense weight of the knowledge he was imparting. "Precisely. The Elder Weavers, in their infinite wisdom, understood that the universe speaks a language of pure essence. They learned to decipher this language, to translate its fundamental truths into symbols that we, in our limited understanding, can grasp. Your locket, child, is a primer, a lexicon of these truths, etched in metal and imbued with the spirit of your ancestors."

He picked up a smooth, dark obsidian shard, similar to the one he had shown her before, but this one bore a different inscription: a sharp, upward-pointing triangle. "This is a Rune of Ascent. It signifies growth, ambition, and the drive to rise above. In the hands of the Weavers, it could be used to imbue an object with the power to defy gravity, to reach heights unimaginable. Or, in its more esoteric application, it could inspire a desperate soul to transcend their limitations."

He then held up a delicate silver disc, etched with a series of flowing, interconnected lines that resembled rippling water. "This is the Rune of Flow. It embodies adaptability, grace, and the ability to navigate challenges without breaking. Imagine its power when woven into a warrior's armor, allowing them to evade blows with uncanny agility. Or consider its application in diplomacy, enabling one to speak with a persuasive fluidity that sways even the most hardened hearts."

Elara found herself mesmerized, her eyes darting between the runes, trying to absorb not just their shapes but the feelings they evoked. The Argent Archive had provided her with the framework, the grammar of runic magic, but Borin was teaching her the poetry, the soul of it. He explained how each rune was a nexus of energy, a focal point where the raw, untamed forces of existence could be directed and shaped.

"The script on your locket is a complex tapestry," Borin continued, his gaze drifting to the intricate symbols that graced her amulet. "It is not a simple sequence of words, but a narrative woven from these fundamental truths. There are runes of lineage, grounding you to your ancestry. There are runes of protection, shielding you from harm. And there are runes, Elara, that speak of awakening, of potential yet unrealized."

He gestured towards a rough, grey stone with a rune that resembled an open hand, palm facing outwards. "This is a Rune of Reception. It is the willingness to receive, to accept, to be open to what is offered. The Weavers used this to create conduits, to draw power from the earth or the stars. On your locket, it likely signifies your inherent ability to absorb and process the runic energies, a testament to your bloodline's affinity for this magic."

Then, he pointed to a rune that looked like a stylized eye, seemingly gazing outward. "This is the Rune of Observation. It speaks of perception, of understanding, of seeing beyond the superficial. It allows one to perceive truths hidden from ordinary sight. Coupled with the Rune of Reception, it suggests your locket is designed to not only absorb energy but to interpret it, to allow you to *understand* the magic you encounter."

Elara closed her eyes, focusing on the locket. She could feel the subtle vibrations of the runes against her skin, a chorus of ancient whispers. She tried to recall the visions she had experienced – the luminous cities, the ethereal beings, the impossible architecture. Were those just dreams, or were they echoes of the truths the runes represented?

"The visions are not mere dreams, child," Borin said, as if he could read her thoughts. "They are the resonance of these primal forces within your spirit. The Elder Weavers did not just inscribe runes onto objects; they etched them onto their very souls. They learned to embody the runes, to become living embodiments of their essence. Your lineage carries that imprint, that deep-seated connection to the cosmic language."

He then presented her with a flat, dark piece of wood, its surface smooth and unblemished. "Now," he said, a glint in his ancient eyes, "we begin the practice. Take this wood. Feel its nature. It is born of the earth, sustained by sunlight and rain, a testament to the slow, deliberate cycle of growth and decay. What rune, Elara, do you feel would best be carved upon it, to honor its essence?"

Elara held the wood, its subtle grain a testament to its living origins. She thought of the runes Borin had shown her, the concepts they represented. She felt a pull towards something that spoke of rootedness, of enduring strength. "The Rune of Stasis?" she suggested hesitantly.

Borin shook his head slowly. "Stasis implies an absence of change, a stillness that can lead to death. This wood is alive, Elara. It grows, it adapts. While Stasis can be a component, it is not its primary truth. Consider the essence of life, of enduring presence."

Elara's mind raced. She recalled the Rune of Ascent, the drive to grow. But this wood was already grown, already established. Then, her gaze fell upon the locket, and a specific symbol seemed to glow in her mind's eye: a simple, circular rune, denoting wholeness, completion.

"The Rune of Wholeness?" she offered, her voice gaining confidence. "It speaks of completeness, of being fully realized."

Borin's weathered face broke into a rare, almost imperceptible smile. "Indeed. The Rune of Wholeness. It speaks of the cycle, of the interconnectedness of all things. It acknowledges the past from which it came, the present it embodies, and the future it will grow into. A wise choice, child. Now, feel the wood. Feel its grain. Imagine the Rune of Wholeness being born from its very being."

He handed her a finely pointed stylus, its tip gleaming like polished bone. "Hold it as you would hold a part of yourself. Let your intention flow through it. Do not force it. Guide it. The rune must emerge from the wood, not be imposed upon it."

With trembling hands, Elara began to trace the circular rune onto the wood. It was a delicate process. She had to feel the resistance of the wood, to sense where it yielded and where it held firm. She channeled the feeling of wholeness, of enduring cycles, into her movements. The stylus seemed to become an extension of her will, the wood a willing participant. As she completed the final curve, a faint, golden light emanated from the inscribed rune, a soft glow that pulsed with a gentle rhythm.

"You see?" Borin rasped, his eyes fixed on the glowing rune. "It is not merely an etching. It is an invocation. The wood now *is* Wholeness, in its own way. It carries that essence, that truth."

Over the following days, Borin guided Elara through a series of similar exercises. He provided her with different materials: a fragment of rough granite, a piece of polished copper, a sliver of moonstone. Each material had its own inherent energies, its own resonant frequencies. He taught her to identify these properties, to understand how they would interact with the runes she chose to carve.

With the granite, he had her carve a Rune of Stability, its sharp, grounded lines mirroring the stone's inherent strength. The resulting rune pulsed with a deep, earthy vibration, grounding Elara whenever she held it. With the copper, he guided her in inscribing a Rune of Communication, its intricate, branching patterns designed to facilitate the exchange of thoughts and ideas. When she finished, the copper felt strangely alive, buzzing with a latent energy that hinted at whispered conversations.

The moonstone proved to be the most challenging. Its ethereal nature resisted forceful inscription. Borin explained that it resonated with intuition, with dreams, with the unseen currents of magic. For this, he had her carve a Rune of Revelation, a symbol that hinted at hidden truths and nascent potential. It required a subtler touch, a deeper connection to her inner senses. As she worked, she felt a tingling sensation spread through her fingertips, and the moonstone seemed to absorb the light around it, glowing with an inner luminescence.

"Each rune has its own voice," Borin explained, gesturing to the collection of carved objects that were beginning to fill a shelf. "The Rune of Wholeness whispers of completion. The Rune of Stability shouts of endurance. The Rune of Communication hums with connection. The Rune of Revelation sighs with secrets unveiled. Your locket contains a symphony of these voices, Elara. To understand it, you must learn to listen to each instrument, and then to the entire orchestra."

He then returned his attention to the locket, which Elara wore constantly. "The symbols here are not arbitrary. They are a precisely crafted sequence, designed to unfold in a particular order, to unlock specific abilities. The locket is a map, and each rune is a landmark, guiding you towards a destination of immense power."

He pointed to a complex, interwoven rune that seemed to shimmer at the edge of Elara's vision. "This, for instance, is a form of the Rune of Binding. But it is not the simple binding of objects, nor even of minds. This is a rune of soul-binding, a glyph that speaks of the deep, unbreakable connection between kindred spirits, between a lineage and its inheritors."

He then traced a series of smaller, seemingly simpler runes that surrounded it. "These are runes of lineage. They are the markers that identify you, that claim you as a descendant of the Elder Weavers. They speak of your heritage, of the magical blood that flows through your veins."

Elara felt a surge of understanding. The locket was not just a collection of symbols; it was a living testament to her identity, a story etched in metal, waiting to be read. She focused her intent, trying to feel the resonance of each rune, to decipher their individual meanings within the larger narrative. The Rune of Reception allowed her to feel the subtle ebb and flow of their power, while the

Rune of Observation helped her to perceive their underlying purpose.

"And this," Borin said, indicating a rune that resembled a nascent star, "is a Rune of Potential. It signifies the untapped power within you, the promise of what you can become. It is a beacon, drawing forth the dormant magic of your ancestors, preparing it for release."

He then presented her with a simple, unadorned bronze pendant. "Now, your turn. I want you to choose a rune that speaks to you, one that resonates with your current needs or desires. Then, imbue it into this pendant. Remember, it is not just about carving the symbol, but about channeling your will, your intent, into the metal."

Elara's mind drifted to the challenges that lay ahead, the unknown dangers that still lurked in the shadows. She thought of the need for strength, for resilience. Her gaze fell upon a rune that represented an unbreakable shield, a glyph of steadfast defense. "The Rune of Aegis," she murmured, feeling its protective energy resonate within her.

She took the bronze pendant and the stylus. Closing her eyes, she pictured the Rune of Aegis, its powerful lines forming a barrier against all threats. She felt the metal warm beneath her touch, and with steady hands, she began to carve. She focused her will, her intention, into the act, pouring her desire for protection into the emerging symbol. As she completed the final stroke, the rune on the pendant flared with a brief, silver light, radiating a tangible sense of security.

Borin nodded, his eyes appraising her work. "Good. You are beginning to understand. The runes are not inert carvings; they are living conduits of power. They are the language of creation, and you, Elara, are learning to speak it." He picked up the Aegis pendant, his calloused fingers tracing the newly formed rune. "This will serve you well. But remember, true mastery lies not just in inscribing the runes, but in understanding the balance. The rune of

96

Aegis provides protection, but it can also foster complacency. The rune of Ascent drives one forward, but it can lead to recklessness. Every glyph has its light and its shadow, its strength and its potential weakness."

He then returned to his workbench, gathering a small collection of objects: a smooth river stone, a shard of volcanic glass, and a twisted piece of ironwood. "The script on your locket," he explained, "is a testament to the Elder Weavers' understanding of this balance. It contains runes of power, yes, but also runes of restraint, of wisdom, of the careful application of force. To truly decipher it, you must look beyond the individual symbols and see the intricate weave of their interplay."

He placed the river stone before her. "This stone carries the essence of water – its fluidity, its adaptability, its ability to wear away even the hardest rock. What rune, then, would complement its nature, allowing you to harness its power without being consumed by it?"

Elara considered the stone, its smooth, cool surface. She thought of the Rune of Flow, but also of its potential to erode, to dissolve. She needed something that would grant her control, that would allow her to direct that fluidity. Her gaze drifted to the locket, to a rune that resembled a carefully placed hand, guiding a stream. "The Rune of Direction?" she proposed. "To channel the flow?"

Borin's smile returned, a subtle widening of his lips. "Precisely. The Rune of Direction. It allows one to guide, to command, to shape the inherent nature of things. Together, the Rune of Flow and the Rune of Direction create a powerful synergy, allowing for controlled, purposeful change."

He then handed her the volcanic glass. "This material is born of fire, of intense heat and pressure. It embodies raw, untamed energy. How would you temper that power, so it serves you, rather than destroying you?"

Elara thought of the locket again, of the runes that seemed to denote a calming influence, a tempering of extremes. She recalled a symbol that looked like a gentle hand placed over a flickering flame. "The Rune of Temperance?" she ventured.

"Excellent," Borin said, his voice laced with approval. "The Rune of Temperance. It acknowledges the power but imposes control, wisdom, and restraint. Imagine the applications, child: controlling the destructive force of fire, or tempering an overwhelming emotion."

Finally, he presented her with the ironwood, a dark, twisted piece of timber that seemed to absorb the light. "This wood is known for its resilience, its resistance to decay. It is stubborn, unyielding. What rune would allow you to work with its nature, rather than against it, to unlock its hidden potential?"

Elara felt a sense of stubbornness emanating from the wood, a refusal to be easily shaped. She thought of the runes that represented persistence, that spoke of overcoming obstacles. Her mind settled on a symbol that looked like a root digging deep into the earth, anchoring itself firmly. "The Rune of Tenacity?" she suggested.

"Indeed," Borin confirmed. "The Rune of Tenacity. It speaks of endurance, of unwavering resolve, of the ability to persevere through hardship. Paired with the inherent resilience of the ironwood, it creates an object imbued with an almost unbreakable will."

As they worked, Borin delved deeper into the history of the Elder Weavers, weaving tales of their mastery and their profound understanding of the runic language. He spoke of how they didn't just carve runes; they *sang* them into existence, their voices imbued with the power of the primal forces they sought to command. He described how they could shape mountains with a whispered rune, command the tides with a chanted glyph, and even influence the very passage of time with intricate runic sequences.

"The script on your locket," Borin explained, his voice growing hushed with reverence, "is a remnant of that ancient artistry. It is a condensed form, a pocket lexicon of the Great Runes, the primal symbols from which all others are derived. Your ancestors were not just users of runes; they were architects of reality, speaking directly to the fundamental forces of existence."

He pointed to a particularly intricate symbol on Elara's locket, one that seemed to swirl with inner light. "This," he said, "is a fragment of the Rune of Becoming. It is the glyph of transformation, of potential unleashed, of the inherent ability to change and evolve. It is the rune that allows for creation, for growth, for the very act of shaping one's destiny."

He then indicated another, a sharp, angular mark that seemed to hum with contained power. "And this... this is a shard of the Rune of Binding. It speaks of connection, of unity, of the forces that hold existence together. In its most profound form, it binds souls, forging bonds that transcend time and space. On your locket, it likely signifies the unbreakable link between you and your lineage, and perhaps, the potential to forge new bonds of power."

Elara felt a profound sense of connection to these concepts, a deep resonance that went beyond mere intellectual understanding. The runes were not just symbols; they were echoes of her own being, reflections of the inherent magic that pulsed within her. The locket, once a beautiful but mysterious artifact, was slowly revealing itself as a key, a guide, and a testament to the extraordinary legacy she carried. Borin's patient tutelage, combined with the growing attunement she felt with the locket, was unraveling the intricate tapestry of her heritage, rune by painstaking rune.

The air in Borin's sanctum, once filled with the quiet hum of potential, now thrummed with a focused intensity. Elara's hands, usually steady, trembled slightly as she held the smooth, unadorned bronze pendant Borin had provided. The locket, nestled against her chest, felt like a heartbeat, a constant reminder of the ancient power that flowed through her veins. The stones Borin had laid out earlier—each a vessel for a concept, a truth made manifest—seemed to watch her, their carved runes silent witnesses to the nascent magic stirring within. She had spent days tracing their forms, feeling their essence, learning to decipher the subtle language of the Elder Weavers. Now, it was time to move beyond mere comprehension, to the art of creation.

Borin's gnarled finger, surprisingly gentle, tapped the pendant Elara held. "This," he rasped, his voice a low, resonant rumble, "is your canvas. The runes we have studied are your pigments. The energy within you, the very spark of your lineage, is your brush. Today, you will paint your first stroke."

Elara swallowed, her throat dry. She had practiced the motions, the visualizations, the channeling of intent. Borin had guided her through inscribing runes onto various materials, each exercise a stepping stone. The Rune of Wholeness on the wood, the Rune of Stability on the granite, the Rune of Communication on the copper, the Rune of Revelation on the moonstone – each had been a lesson in focus and directed will. But those had been more akin to imprinting existing energies onto receptive mediums. This was different. This was to *create* energy, to weave it into existence, to shape it with her own burgeoning power.

"The script on your locket," Borin continued, his gaze fixed on the intricate symbols adorning her own amulet, "is a symphony. Each rune plays its part, contributing to the grand composition of your heritage. Today, you will compose a single note. A simple, yet vital one. You will cast a ward."

A ward. The concept settled into her mind, solidifying the abstract notions of protective magic. It was a shield, a barrier, a subtle redirection of unwanted forces. Borin had shown her the Rune of Aegis, the unyielding shield, and the Rune of Temperance, the gentle hand that calmed wild flames. But for a ward against minor dark influences, something more nuanced was needed – a subtle redirection, a subtle repulsion.

"I will use," Elara began, her voice gaining a touch of her usual resolve, "a combination. The Rune of Observation, to perceive and identify the influence, and a modified Rune of Repulsion, to deter it without brute force."

Borin nodded, a flicker of approval in his ancient eyes. "A wise choice. Over-reliance on raw power can be a blunt instrument, easily blunted or turned against the wielder. Subtlety has its own strength. Now, focus. Feel the energy within you, the echo of your ancestors. It is not a separate entity to be summoned, but an intrinsic part of your being, waiting to be directed."

Elara closed her eyes, letting out a slow, steady breath. She felt the familiar warmth of the locket against her skin, a subtle anchor. Then, she reached inward, not forcing, but *inviting*. She envisioned the currents of energy within her, like a hidden river flowing beneath the surface of her consciousness. It felt warm, vibrant, pulsing with a life of its own. She remembered the Rune of Reception Borin had described, the glyph that allowed one to accept and process energies. She focused on that sensation, allowing the inner river to become more defined, more accessible.

Next, she called to mind the Rune of Observation. Not the static carving, but its essence: clarity, perception, the ability to see beyond the veil. She imagined her mind's eye sharpening, attuned to the subtle dissonances that marked the presence of a dark influence. She pictured a gentle, golden light emanating from her consciousness, a delicate probe, sensing the edges of the unseen.

"The ward does not merely repel," Borin's voice, calm and steady, guided her. "It understands. It *knows* what it is warning against. This allows for a precise and efficient application of force, minimizing any unwanted collateral effects."

Elara continued to focus, the image of the ward solidifying in her mind. It wasn't a solid wall, but rather a shimmering, almost invisible field. For the repulsion aspect, she envisioned a gentle, wave-like motion emanating from the pendant, like ripples spreading across still water. It was the Rune of Flow, but applied not to the element itself, but to the energy of repulsion. A subtle nudge, rather than a forceful shove.

She visualized the Rune of Observation as a finely etched lens at the center of the ward, and the modified Rune of Repulsion as the shimmering, wave-like boundary. She felt the energies coalesce, a delicate dance between perception and redirection. The bronze pendant in her hand grew warmer, a tangible manifestation of the magic she was carefully weaving.

"Now, the inscription," Borin instructed softly. "Do not carve *onto* the pendant, Elara. Let the rune *emerge from* it. Imagine the metal itself resonating with the chosen symbols. Feel the runes becoming one with the bronze."

Taking a deep breath, Elara focused on the pendant. She saw, in her mind's eye, the Rune of Observation forming on its surface, not as a physical etching, but as a shimmering imprint of light. She channeled the feeling of clarity, of discerning truth, into the metal. The bronze seemed to absorb the intention, a faint glow emanating from its surface. It was a subtle process, requiring immense concentration. She felt the faint resistance of the metal, not as an obstacle, but as a guide, shaping the intangible energy.

Then, she moved to the Rune of Repulsion. This was more challenging. It wasn't a single, static symbol, but a dynamic intent. She visualized the wave-like motion, the gentle pushing away of negativity. She poured her desire for protection, for safety, into the pendant. The bronze pulsed, a slow, rhythmic beat that mirrored the nascent power within her. She felt a tingling sensation spread from her fingertips up her arms, a sign that the energy was flowing, that the enchantment was taking hold.

For what felt like an eternity, she held the pendant, her entire being focused on the delicate act of creation. She poured her will, her nascent understanding of the runic language, into the bronze. It was an exercise in patience and precision, a stark contrast to the raw, untamed power she had felt in glimpses before. This was controlled creation, a testament to her growing mastery.

Slowly, painstakingly, the ward began to manifest. It was not visible to the naked eye, but Elara could *feel* it. A subtle pressure around the pendant, a faint hum that resonated with her own heartbeat. It was a protective shell, spun from her own energy and guided by the ancient wisdom of the runes. The feeling was unlike anything she had experienced before – a profound sense of accomplishment, a deep satisfaction that settled into her bones.

Borin watched her, his face impassive, but Elara could sense his keen observation. He wasn't judging, but assessing, ensuring that the process was correct, that the intention was pure. Finally, as Elara felt the energy stabilize, the subtle hum deepening into a steady thrum, she released her focus.

She opened her eyes and met Borin's gaze. He nodded, a rare, genuine smile gracing his lips. "It is done."

Elara looked down at the pendant. It appeared unchanged, still a simple piece of bronze. Yet, she knew otherwise. She could feel the latent power within it, a gentle ward against the shadows. She held it out, and Borin took it, his rough fingers brushing hers. He closed his eyes, his brow furrowed in concentration. A moment later, he opened them, a faint frown marring his features.

"There is a whisper," he said, his voice thoughtful. "A faint disturbance on the periphery of the ward. A minor shadow, drawn by the very act of creation. It probes, seeking weakness."

Elara's heart leaped into her throat. Had she failed?

"Do not be alarmed," Borin continued, seeing her distress. "This is expected. The act of creating magic often attracts the attention of those who dwell in its absence. Your ward is holding firm. It is not a fortress, but a well-maintained gate. It repels, it deflects, it reassures the bearer of its presence."

He then placed the pendant back into her hand. "Now, test it yourself. Hold it. Feel its presence. Imagine a dark thought, a fleeting moment of malice, reaching out towards you. Feel how the ward reacts."

Elara took the pendant, its warmth now a comforting presence. She closed her eyes and deliberately summoned a dark thought, a sliver of doubt, a whisper of fear. She focused on the feeling of being exposed, vulnerable. As the negative intent coalesced in her mind, she felt a subtle shift around the pendant. It was like a gentle pressure pushing back, a soft sigh of resistance. The dark thought, instead of taking root, seemed to dissipate, unable to penetrate the subtle shield.

A thrill coursed through her. It was real. She had consciously shaped energy, woven runes into a tangible effect. It was a small ward, a minor enchantment, but it was *hers*. It was proof that the knowledge Borin imparted, the ancestral magic she carried, was not just theory, but a force she could wield.

"The Rune of Observation recognized the malice," Borin explained, his voice resonating with quiet authority. "It noted its nature, its intent. Then, the modified Rune of Repulsion responded, not with a violent expulsion, but with a gentle redirection. It nudged the negative energy away, like a skilled dancer sidestepping an opponent's clumsy lunge."

He gestured to the collection of carved objects on the shelf – the wood, the granite, the copper, the moonstone. "Those were lessons in understanding the potential of runes, in learning to imbue them into receptive materials. This," he tapped the pendant, "is a lesson in activation, in the conscious channeling of your own innate power. You have taken a concept, a theoretical application, and made it manifest."

Elara clutched the pendant, its warmth spreading through her palm. The exhilaration was intoxicating. It was more than just a magical achievement; it was a validation of her journey, a testament to her growing connection with her heritage. She had always felt the magic within her, a distant hum, a promise. Now, she had taken that promise and given it form.

"It feels… solid," she breathed, a wide smile gracing her lips. "I can feel its presence. It's like an extension of myself."

"That is the goal," Borin said, his eyes twinkling. "The runes are not external tools, Elara. There are ways to articulate, to focus, and to amplify the magic that is already within you. The Elder Weavers did not simply *use* runes; they *embodied* them. They became living conduits of their essence. Your locket, the script upon it, is designed to facilitate that embodiment, to guide you on that path."

He picked up a small, unadorned stone, its surface smooth and grey. "Now, this stone. It speaks of stillness, of patience. Of the quiet strength found in enduring. What rune would you imbue it with, to reflect that essence?"

Elara looked at the stone, feeling its quiet solidity. She thought of the runes they had discussed – the Rune of Stasis, representing permanence, and the Rune of Tenacity, representing perseverance. But this stone felt different; it wasn't stagnant, but rather possessed a deep, unwavering calm.

"The Rune of Serenity?" she ventured, picturing a gentle, flowing line, encompassing a still point at its center. "A peace that is not born of inaction, but of deep inner balance."

Borin turned the stone over in his hand, his gaze thoughtful. "Serenity. A potent concept. And a necessary one. For true power, Elara, lies not in the force one wields, but in the control one maintains. The ability to remain calm amidst chaos, to find stillness in the storm. Yes, Serenity is a fitting choice. Now, show me how you would weave that concept into this stone."

He handed her a fine-pointed stylus. Elara took it, feeling its cool, smooth texture. She held the stone, letting its quiet essence seep into her. She visualized the Rune of Serenity, not as a sharp inscription, but as a gentle embrace. She focused on the feeling of peace, of unwavering calm, and began to trace the rune onto the stone. It was not about forcing the shape, but about coaxing it, allowing the stone to reveal the rune that already lay dormant within its being.

As she completed the final curve of the symbol, a soft, luminous glow emanated from the stone, a gentle, ethereal light that seemed to soothe the very air around them. The glow pulsed softly, a silent testament to the successful enchantment.

"You see," Borin rasped, a note of deep satisfaction in his voice. "Each material, each rune, each intention – they all combine to create something new, something imbued with purpose. Your first intentional enchantment, Elara, was a success. It marks a turning point. You have moved from understanding the language of magic to speaking it."

He placed the now glowing stone in Elara's palm. It felt cool, yet pulsed with a gentle warmth, a tangible symbol of her achievement. "The path of runes is long and arduous, child. But with each inscription, each successful enchantment, you draw closer to understanding the immense power that lies within you, and within the world around you. This ward, this stone of Serenity – they are but the first steps. Many more await."

Elara looked at the pendant and the stone, her heart swelling with a quiet triumph. The fear and uncertainty that had often clouded her journey began to recede, replaced by a burgeoning sense of self-belief. The runes, once abstract symbols, were now becoming living entities, extensions of her will, reflections of her growing power. The journey was indeed long, but for the first time, Elara felt truly ready to embrace its every step. The path of runes was no longer a distant, daunting prospect, but a tangible reality, a language she was finally learning to speak, and more importantly, to understand. She was no longer just a student of magic; she was a wielder of it.

The air in Borin's sanctum, once filled with the quiet hum of potential, now thrummed with a focused intensity. Elara's hands, usually steady, trembled slightly as she held the smooth, unadorned bronze pendant Borin had provided. The locket, nestled against her chest, felt like a heartbeat, a constant reminder of the ancient power that flowed through her veins. The stones Borin had laid out earlier—each a vessel for a concept, a truth made manifest—seemed to watch her, their carved runes silent witnesses to the nascent magic stirring within. She had spent days tracing their forms, feeling their essence, learning to decipher the subtle language of the Elder Weavers. Now, it was time to move beyond mere comprehension, to the art of creation.

Borin's gnarled finger, surprisingly gentle, tapped the pendant Elara held. "This," he rasped, his voice a low, resonant rumble, "is your canvas. The runes we have studied are your pigments. The energy within you, the very spark of your lineage, is your brush. Today, you will paint your first stroke."

Elara swallowed, her throat dry. She had practiced the motions, the visualizations, the channeling of intent. Borin had guided her through inscribing runes onto various materials, each exercise a stepping stone. The Rune of Wholeness on the wood, the Rune of Stability on the granite, the Rune of Communication on the copper, the Rune of Revelation on the moonstone – each had been a lesson in focus and directed will. But those had been more akin to imprinting existing energies onto receptive mediums. This was different. This was to *create* energy, to weave it into existence, to shape it with her own burgeoning power.

"The script on your locket," Borin continued, his gaze fixed on the intricate symbols adorning her own amulet, "is a symphony. Each rune plays its part, contributing to the grand composition of your heritage. Today, you will compose a single note. A simple, yet vital one. You will cast a ward."

A ward. The concept settled into her mind, solidifying the abstract notions of protective magic. It was a shield, a barrier, a subtle redirection of unwanted forces. Borin had shown her the Rune of Aegis, the unyielding shield, and the Rune of Temperance, the gentle hand that calmed wild flames. But for a ward against minor dark influences, something more nuanced was needed – a subtle redirection, a subtle repulsion.

"I will use," Elara began, her voice gaining a touch of her usual resolve, "a combination. The Rune of Observation, to perceive and identify the influence, and a modified Rune of Repulsion, to deter it without brute force."

Borin nodded, a flicker of approval in his ancient eyes. "A wise choice. Over-reliance on raw power can be a blunt instrument, easily blunted or turned against the wielder. Subtlety has its own strength. Now, focus. Feel the energy within you, the echo of your ancestors. It is not a separate entity to be summoned, but an intrinsic part of your being, waiting to be directed."

Elara closed her eyes, letting out a slow, steady breath. She felt the familiar warmth of the locket against her skin, a subtle anchor. Then, she reached inward, not forcing, but *inviting*. She envisioned the currents of energy within her, like a hidden river flowing beneath the surface of her consciousness. It felt warm, vibrant, pulsing with a life of its own. She remembered the Rune of Reception Borin had described, the glyph that allowed one to accept and process energies. She focused on that sensation, allowing the inner river to become more defined, more accessible.

Next, she called to mind the Rune of Observation. Not the static carving, but its essence: clarity, perception, the ability to see beyond the veil. She imagined her mind's eye sharpening, attuned to the subtle dissonances that marked the presence of a dark influence. She pictured a gentle, golden light emanating from her consciousness, a delicate probe, sensing the edges of the unseen.

"The ward does not merely repel," Borin's voice, calm and steady, guided her. "It understands. It *knows* what it is warning against. This allows for a precise and efficient application of force, minimizing any unwanted collateral effects."

Elara continued to focus, the image of the ward solidifying in her mind. It wasn't a solid wall, but rather a shimmering, almost invisible field. For the repulsion aspect, she envisioned a gentle, wave-like motion emanating from the pendant, like ripples spreading across still water. It was the Rune of Flow, but applied not to the element itself, but to the energy of repulsion. A subtle nudge, rather than a forceful shove.

She visualized the Rune of Observation as a finely etched lens at the center of the ward, and the modified Rune of Repulsion as the shimmering, wave-like boundary. She felt the energies coalesce, a delicate dance between perception and redirection. The bronze pendant in her hand grew warmer, a tangible manifestation of the magic she was carefully weaving.

"Now, the inscription," Borin instructed softly. "Do not carve *onto* the pendant, Elara. Let the rune *emerge from* it. Imagine the metal itself resonating with the chosen symbols. Feel the runes becoming one with the bronze."

Taking a deep breath, Elara focused on the pendant. She saw, in her mind's eye, the Rune of Observation forming on its surface, not as a physical etching, but as a shimmering imprint of light. She channeled the feeling of clarity, of discerning truth, into the metal. The bronze seemed to absorb the intention, a faint glow emanating from its surface. It was a subtle process, requiring immense concentration. She felt the faint resistance of the metal, not as an obstacle, but as a guide, shaping the intangible energy.

Then, she moved to the Rune of Repulsion. This was more challenging. It wasn't a single, static symbol, but a dynamic intent. She visualized the wave-like motion, the gentle pushing away of negativity. She poured her desire for protection, for safety, into the pendant. The bronze pulsed, a slow, rhythmic beat that mirrored the nascent power within her. She felt a tingling sensation spread from her fingertips up her arms, a sign that the energy was flowing, that the enchantment was taking hold.

For what felt like an eternity, she held the pendant, her entire being focused on the delicate act of creation. She poured her will, her nascent understanding of the runic language, into the bronze. It was an exercise in patience and precision, a stark contrast to the raw, untamed power she had felt in glimpses before. This was controlled creation, a testament to her growing mastery.

Slowly, painstakingly, the ward began to manifest. It was not visible to the naked eye, but Elara could *feel* it. A subtle pressure around the pendant, a faint hum that resonated with her own heartbeat. It was a protective shell, spun from her own energy and guided by the ancient wisdom of the runes. The feeling was unlike anything she had experienced before – a profound sense of accomplishment, a deep satisfaction that settled into her bones.

Borin watched her, his face impassive, but Elara could sense his keen observation. He wasn't judging, but assessing, ensuring that the process was correct, that the intention was pure. Finally, as Elara felt the energy stabilize, the subtle hum deepening into a steady thrum, she released her focus.

She opened her eyes and met Borin's gaze. He nodded, a rare, genuine smile gracing his lips. "It is done."

Elara looked down at the pendant. It appeared unchanged, still a simple piece of bronze. Yet, she knew otherwise. She could feel the latent power within it, a gentle ward against the shadows. She held it out, and Borin took it, his rough fingers brushing hers. He closed his eyes, his brow furrowed in concentration. A moment later, he opened them, a faint frown marring his features.

"There is a whisper," he said, his voice thoughtful. "A faint disturbance on the periphery of the ward. A minor shadow, drawn by the very act of creation. It probes, seeking weakness."

Elara's heart leaped into her throat. Had she failed?

"Do not be alarmed," Borin continued, seeing her distress. "This is expected. The act of creating magic often attracts the attention of those who dwell in its absence. Your ward is holding firm. It is not a fortress, but a well-maintained gate. It repels, it deflects, it reassures the bearer of its presence."

He then placed the pendant back into her hand. "Now, test it yourself. Hold it. Feel its presence. Imagine a dark thought, a fleeting moment of malice, reaching out towards you. Feel how the ward reacts."

Elara took the pendant, its warmth now a comforting presence. She closed her eyes and deliberately summoned a dark thought, a sliver of doubt, a whisper of fear. She focused on the feeling of being exposed, vulnerable. As the negative intent coalesced in her mind, she felt a subtle shift around the pendant. It was like a gentle pressure pushing back, a soft sigh of resistance. The dark thought, instead of taking root, seemed to dissipate, unable to penetrate the subtle shield.

A thrill coursed through her. It was real. She had consciously shaped energy, woven runes into a tangible effect. It was a small ward, a minor enchantment, but it was *hers*. It was proof that the knowledge Borin imparted, the ancestral magic she carried, was not just theory, but a force she could wield.

"The Rune of Observation recognized the malice," Borin explained, his voice resonating with quiet authority. "It noted its nature, its intent. Then, the modified Rune of Repulsion responded, not with a violent expulsion, but with a gentle redirection. It nudged the negative energy away, like a skilled dancer sidestepping an opponent's clumsy lunge."

He gestured to the collection of carved objects on the shelf – the wood, the granite, the copper, the moonstone. "Those were lessons in understanding the potential of runes, in learning to imbue them into receptive materials. This," he tapped the pendant, "is a lesson in activation, in the conscious channeling of your own innate power. You have taken a concept, a theoretical application, and made it manifest."

Elara clutched the pendant, its warmth spreading through her palm. The exhilaration was intoxicating. It was more than just a magical achievement; it was a validation of her journey, a testament to her growing connection with her heritage. She had always felt the magic within her, a distant hum, a promise. Now, she had taken that promise and given it form.

"It feels… solid," she breathed, a wide smile gracing her lips. "I can feel its presence. It's like an extension of myself."

"That is the goal," Borin said, his eyes twinkling. "The runes are not external tools, Elara. There are ways to articulate, to focus, and to amplify the magic that is already within you. The Elder Weavers did not simply *use* runes; they *embodied* them. They became living conduits of their essence. Your locket, the script upon it, is designed to facilitate that embodiment, to guide you on that path."

112

He picked up a small, unadorned stone, its surface smooth and grey. "Now, this stone. It speaks of stillness, of patience. Of the quiet strength found in enduring. What rune would you imbue it with, to reflect that essence?"

Elara looked at the stone, feeling its quiet solidity. She thought of the runes they had discussed – the Rune of Stasis, representing permanence, and the Rune of Tenacity, representing perseverance. But this stone felt different; it wasn't stagnant, but rather possessed a deep, unwavering calm.

"The Rune of Serenity?" she ventured, picturing a gentle, flowing line, encompassing a still point at its center. "A peace that is not born of inaction, but of deep inner balance."

Borin turned the stone over in his hand, his gaze thoughtful. "Serenity. A potent concept. And a necessary one. For true power, Elara, lies not in the force one wields, but in the control one maintains. The ability to remain calm amidst chaos, to find stillness in the storm. Yes, Serenity is a fitting choice. Now, show me how you would weave that concept into this stone."

He handed her a fine-pointed stylus. Elara took it, feeling its cool, smooth texture. She held the stone, letting its quiet essence seep into her. She visualized the Rune of Serenity, not as a sharp inscription, but as a gentle embrace. She focused on the feeling of peace, of unwavering calm, and began to trace the rune onto the stone. It was not about forcing the shape, but about coaxing it, allowing the stone to reveal the rune that already lay dormant within its being.

As she completed the final curve of the symbol, a soft, luminous glow emanated from the stone, a gentle, ethereal light that seemed to soothe the very air around them. The glow pulsed softly, a silent testament to the successful enchantment.

"You see," Borin rasped, a note of deep satisfaction in his voice. "Each material, each rune, each intention – they all combine to create something new, something imbued with purpose. Your first intentional enchantment, Elara, was a success. It marks a turning point. You have moved from understanding the language of magic to speaking it."

He placed the now glowing stone in Elara's palm. It felt cool, yet pulsed with a gentle warmth, a tangible symbol of her achievement. "The path of runes is long and arduous, child. But with each inscription, each successful enchantment, you draw closer to understanding the immense power that lies within you, and within the world around you. This ward, this stone of Serenity – they are but the first steps. Many more await."

Elara looked at the pendant and the stone, her heart swelling with a quiet triumph. The fear and uncertainty that had often clouded her journey began to recede, replaced by a burgeoning sense of self-belief. The runes, once abstract symbols, were now becoming living entities, extensions of her will, reflections of her growing power. The journey was indeed long, but for the first time, Elara felt truly ready to embrace its every step. The path of runes was no longer a distant, daunting prospect, but a tangible reality, a language she was finally learning to speak, and more importantly, to understand. She was no longer just a student of magic; she was a wielder of it.

The newfound confidence, however, was a fragile bloom, easily overshadowed by the encroaching tendrils of darkness. It began subtly, as it always did. A fleeting chill that had nothing to do with the ambient temperature, a prickling sensation on the back of her neck that suggested unseen observation. At first, Elara dismissed it as the lingering effects of her training, the heightened sensitivity that came with awakening her inherent magic. But the feeling persisted, growing more insistent, more unnerving.

One evening, as she practiced the intricate hand gestures for a healing cantrip Borin had taught her – the Rune of Restoration, a delicate intertwining of lines that mimicked the mending of torn fabric – she felt it again. A cold, predatory stillness seemed to settle in the corners of the room, pressing in from the edges of her vision. Her breath hitched. She faltered in her movements, the luminous threads of energy she was weaving sputtering and dying.

"Did you feel that?" she whispered, her voice tight with a fear she hadn't experienced since the night of her parents' disappearance.

Borin, who had been observing from his usual spot by the hearth, his eyes alight with the dying embers of the fire, turned his head slowly. His gaze, usually filled with a gentle knowing, was sharp, assessing. "Feel what, child?"

"A... a presence," Elara stammered, her eyes darting towards the shadows. "Like something watching. Something cold."

Borin's brow furrowed. He rose slowly, his movements stiff but deliberate, and walked towards the window. He peered out into the twilight gloom, his keen eyes scanning the ancient trees that ringed the small clearing where his cottage stood. The wind rustled the leaves, a mournful sigh that did little to dispel the rising tension in the air.

There is nothing visible," he said at last, his voice carefully neutral. But Elara, now attuned to the subtle shifts in his demeanor, detected a subtle tension in his shoulders, a slight hardening of his jaw. He had felt it too.

Later that night, the whispers began. They were faint at first, like the rustling of dry leaves or the distant murmur of a stream. But as Elara lay in her bed, the Rune of Serenity stone clutched in her hand, the whispers seemed to coalesce, to form a cohesive, chilling thread of sound that slithered just at the edge of her hearing. They spoke of shadows, of hunger, of a thirst for what she carried within her. They were not words, not in any language she knew, but the intent was clear, primal, and terrifying.

She sat bolt upright, her heart hammering against her ribs. The ward on her locket pulsed with a faint warmth against her skin, a small comfort against the growing dread. She looked towards Kael, who slept soundly on his mat by the door, his breathing even and deep. She envied him his peace, his ignorance of the growing danger.

The next morning, Kael was restless. He paced the small cottage, his keen wolf senses seemingly on edge. He whined low in his throat, his golden eyes scanning the surrounding woods with an intensity that mirrored Elara's own growing apprehension.

"What is it, Kael?" Elara asked, stroking his thick, grey fur.

He nudged her hand with his muzzle, then turned his gaze towards the forest's edge. A low growl rumbled in his chest. "He senses it too," Borin said, his voice grave as he entered the main room. "The shadows stir. Your awakening, Elara, has not gone unnoticed."

Borin's words hung in the air, heavy with unspoken meaning. He explained that the bloodline of the Elder Weavers was not merely a repository of ancient magic, but a beacon. A beacon that attracted not only those who sought to understand and wield its power, but also those who feared it, those who sought to extinguish it. Her parents had been guardians of that legacy, and their fate was a stark testament to the lengths to which such entities would go.

"There are those who consider the resurgence of your line a threat," Borin elaborated, his gaze steady and unflinching. "They are ancient, and they are powerful. They fear what you represent – a return to balance, a challenge to their own dominion. They will not hesitate to try and silence you, Elara. Permanently."

The whispers seemed to echo his words in the silence that followed. Elara felt a cold dread seep into her bones. The playful exploration of runes, the quiet satisfaction of her first successful enchantment, now seemed like a dangerous flirtation with forces she couldn't comprehend.

"What can we do?" she asked, her voice barely a whisper.

"We prepare," Borin stated, his resolve hardening. "We train. You must master your abilities, not just to defend yourself, but to understand the enemy. Kael's senses will be invaluable. He can detect their presence long before we can. And your own intuition, your growing connection to the runes, will guide you."

He then produced a small, intricately carved wooden box from a hidden compartment in his workbench. The wood was dark, almost black, and etched with a complex pattern of swirling lines that seemed to shift and writhe with a life of their own. "This," he said, his voice laced with a reverence that Elara had rarely heard, "was your mother's. It holds certain... protections. And perhaps, more than that."

He opened the box, revealing not jewels or treasures, but a collection of smooth, grey stones, each inscribed with a single, deeply carved rune. Elara recognized some of them – the Rune of Warding, the Rune of Silence, the Rune of Obscurity. But others were unfamiliar, their forms alien and unsettling.

"These are keyed to your blood," Borin explained, gesturing to the stones. "They will respond to your touch, to your intent. They are pieces of your mother's legacy, fragments of her power, waiting for you to reclaim them."

As Elara reached out to touch the cool, smooth surface of one of the stones, a distinct feeling of unease washed over her. It wasn't the same cold dread as before, but a disquieting sense of being *known*. As if something, somewhere, had just registered her presence, her burgeoning power, with a chillingly precise awareness. The shadows outside the cottage seemed to deepen, and for the first time, Elara understood that the path of runes was not just a journey of discovery, but a descent into a world where light and shadow were locked in an eternal, perilous struggle. The warning had been issued, not in words, but in the icy touch of unseen presences, and

Elara knew, with a certainty that settled deep in her soul, that the time for passive learning was over. The hunt had begun.

CHAPTER 4:

ECHOES OF THE SUNDERED REALM

Kael's low growl, a sound that vibrated not just in his chest but through the very floorboards of Borin's humble dwelling, was the first indication that something far more profound than mere shadows was at play. The palpable tension in the air, the prickling sensation on Elara's skin, the chilling whispers that had plagued her nights – they were not random manifestations of a nascent magical sensitivity, but the harbingers of a truth far grander and more terrifying. Borin's steady gaze, now fixed upon the wolf-like companion, held a depth of understanding that Elara had not seen before, a silent acknowledgement of the unspoken knowledge Kael possessed.

"The whispers," Kael began, his voice a low rumble that seemed to bypass Elara's ears and resonate directly within her mind, a curious and unsettling phenomenon that amplified the urgency of his words. "They are not merely the echoes of darkness drawn to your awakening. They are tendrils, probing the weak points in the Veil."

The word "Veil" hung in the air, imbued with an immediate significance that transcended its common definition. Elara's mind, still grappling with the recent revelations of her lineage and the predatory forces that now seemed to stalk her every step, struggled to grasp its true meaning. "The Veil?" she echoed, her voice barely a breath.

Borin, ever the stoic anchor in this sea of unfolding mysteries, stepped forward, his gnarled hands clasped before him. "The Veil is the barrier, Elara, the shimmering membrane that separates our world from others. For millennia, your ancestors, the Elder Weavers, were its custodians."

Kael's golden eyes met Elara's, a startling intensity burning within them. "Not just custodians, Elara. They were its architects, its architects, and its guardians. They wove the very fabric of the Veil, ensuring its integrity. It is a realm of potent magic, a dimension woven from the threads of pure arcane energy – a place your bloodline once called home."

Elara's breath hitched. A parallel dimension? A realm of magic where her ancestors had held dominion? It was a concept so vast, so utterly world-altering, that it threatened to shatter the foundations of her understanding. The ancestral magic within her, the burgeoning power that Borin had so carefully begun to nurture, suddenly felt less like a personal inheritance and more like a key – a key to realms unknown, to histories untold.

"The Sundered Realm," Kael elaborated, the name rolling off his mental tongue with a weight of ancient sorrow. "That is what it is called. A place of untamed magic, where the very air crackles with arcane potential. It is intrinsically linked to this world, yet distinct, separated by the Veil. And that Veil… it is not an impenetrable wall. It thins in places where magic is strong, where the echoes of its creation resonate. Places like this." He gestured around Borin's sanctum, a space already imbued with a subtle, potent energy.

Elara's gaze fell upon the locket resting against her chest. Borin had called it a key, attuned to her bloodline. Now, its purpose seemed to expand exponentially. It was not merely a conduit for her own nascent power, but a potential bridge, a means of interacting with this unseen barrier, perhaps even of crossing it. "My parents…" she began, the pain of their loss a familiar ache, now tinged with a dawning comprehension. "They were guardians of this Veil?"

Borin nodded, his expression grim. "They were. And their fate, Elara, is a testament to the dangers inherent in such a role. The Veil is not merely a separation; it is a contested border. And there are forces that seek to tear it down, to breach the barriers and unleash chaos upon both realms."

Kael's mental voice grew sterner, the comforting warmth of his presence now underscored by a chilling urgency. "The entities that whisper to you, they are not of your world. They are creatures of the Sundered Realm, or perhaps something that has found a way to feed on the echoes of its power. They sense the thinning of the Veil, and they sense *you*. You are a Weaver, Elara. A direct descendant of those who shaped the Veil. Your very presence acts as a beacon, drawing their attention like a flame draws moths."

The locket felt warmer against her skin, a tangible connection to this newly revealed tapestry of existence. She ran a finger over its smooth, cool surface, the faint inscription of the runes she had worked so hard to understand now seeming to pulse with a hidden life. If it were a key, what did it unlock? And what lay beyond?

"The Veil thins in places of great power," Borin repeated, his eyes distant as if gazing upon a landscape Elara could not yet perceive. "These thinning points, or 'thinning places,' are not static. They shift and waver, influenced by the ebb and flow of magic, by significant events, and by the presence of those who carry the blood of the Weavers. Your lineage possesses an inherent resonance with the Veil, a deep-seated connection that allows for both its maintenance and, if need be, its traversal."

He then picked up one of the carved stones from his workbench, its surface still bearing the faint imprints of Elara's recent efforts. "Your attempts to weave enchantments, to imbue objects with magical intent, have not gone unnoticed. Each act of creation sends ripples through the ambient energies. For those attuned to such currents, it is like a trumpet call. Your awakening, Elara, has been a signal, a clear indication that a new Weaver has arisen."

Kael shifted his weight, his eyes never leaving Elara. "Your parents understood this. They walked the line between realms, their lives dedicated to ensuring the Veil remained intact. They understood the creatures that lurked in the spaces between, the entities that craved the raw magic of your world, or the potent life force of your own realm. They fought them, Elara, not with brute force, but with the intricate art of the Weavers – shaping energies, redirecting currents, reinforcing the very fabric of reality."

Elara closed her eyes, trying to reconcile the mundane reality of Borin's cottage with the fantastical world Kael was describing. The whispers, the chilling presences, the growing sense of being hunted – it all began to coalesce into a terrifying narrative. Her lineage was not just a source of power; it was a responsibility, a burden that had claimed her parents' lives.

"So, the locket…" she began, her voice gaining a measure of her usual resolve, fueled by a desperate need to understand. "It can interact with this Veil?"

"More than interact, child," Kael's voice was laced with a reverence that belied his lupine form. "It is a key. A nexus point attuned to your bloodline. It can help you perceive the Veil, to sense its presence, and, with sufficient understanding and power, it can allow you to cross it. Your parents imbued it with their knowledge, their intent, and their very essence. It is a legacy, waiting for its rightful heir to awaken its full potential."

Borin nodded in agreement. "The runes you have learned, Elara, are the building blocks of the Veil itself. The Elder Weavers did not merely *use* runes; they *were* runes, living embodiments of their fundamental principles. They understood the deep currents of existence, the interwoven nature of all things. Your training has been to reawaken that understanding within you, to prepare you for the path your ancestors walked."

He gestured towards the window, where the twilight was deepening into a velvety black. "The thinning places are like doorways. Some are stable, requiring specific keys or rituals to open. Others are more volatile, flickering into existence with the surge of powerful magic or the resonance of a Weaver's blood. Your awakening, coupled with the inherent potency of this location, has likely caused a significant thinning, attracting unwelcome attention."

"The darkness you feel," Kael added, his mental voice a low thrum of concern, "is the hunger of these entities. They are drawn to the raw energy of this world, an energy they cannot sustain themselves on. They see your awakening as an opportunity, a chance to exploit the weakened Veil and feast upon what lies beyond."

Elara's fingers tightened around the locket. The small pendant, which had recently represented her first step into the world of magic, now felt like a cosmic artifact of immense significance. It was a link to her past, a tool for her present, and potentially, a gateway to her future – a future that was becoming increasingly perilous.

"Your parents understood the delicate balance," Borin said, his voice soft with a sorrow that spoke of shared loss. "They knew that the Veil was not meant to be a prison, but a sanctuary. A place where the primal energies of the Sundered Realm could exist without overwhelming this world, and where the lifeblood of this world could thrive undisturbed. They dedicated their lives to maintaining that separation, that sacred trust."

Kael let out a soft huff, a sound that was more of a mournful sigh than a vocalization. "They knew the cost. They knew that the forces that opposed them were ancient and relentless. They fought not just for themselves, but for the continued existence of both realms. Their guardianship was a constant, dangerous vigil."

The implications of Kael's words settled upon Elara like a shroud. Her parents hadn't simply disappeared; they had likely fallen in the line of duty, defending a fundamental barrier that protected all life. And now, that same duty, that same peril, was being thrust upon her. The whispers were not just a nuisance; they were a warning. The shadows were not just an abstract threat; they were the scouts of an encroaching darkness.

"The locket," Borin continued, his voice returning to its usual measured tone, though an undercurrent of gravity remained, "is designed to attune to your bloodline. It acts as a focal point, a beacon for the Veil's energies, and a key to navigating its shifting currents. Your mother's imprint is upon it, a guiding hand for you, her daughter, should you choose to walk this path."

He looked at Elara directly, his ancient eyes holding a mixture of stern expectation and deep compassion. "The journey your parents undertook was not one of choice, but of destiny. The blood of the Elder Weavers carries with it a profound responsibility. The Veil needs its guardians, Elara. And with your awakening, you have declared yourself ready, whether you know it or not."

Kael nudged Elara's hand again, a silent reassurance that was both comforting and disconcerting. He was not just a companion; he was a conduit to knowledge, a link to the truth of her heritage. "The Sundered Realm," he reiterated, his mental voice echoing the weight of ages, "is not a place of simple magic. It is a realm of pure creation and potent destruction, a place where your ancestors once held sway, shaping realities with their will. But it is also a realm that is fragile, its balance easily disrupted. And now, it is threatened."

Elara felt a strange calm settle over her, a quiet determination born from the clarity of the danger. The fear was still present, a cold knot in her stomach, but it was now accompanied by a burgeoning sense of purpose. Her parents had died protecting this Veil. She carried their blood, their legacy. She could not turn away.

"The thinning places," Borin explained, his gaze sweeping over the intricate carvings on his workbench, each one a testament to his own deep knowledge of the arcane. "They are points of resonance. Places where the fabric of reality is stretched thin, allowing for interaction between worlds. Your presence, child, amplifies this resonance. The locket will allow you to perceive these thinning places, to sense their instability, and to perhaps even stabilize them, or, as your parents did, to traverse them."

He picked up a shard of what looked like obsidian, polished to a mirror sheen. "Imagine this," he said, holding it out to Elara. "A piece of the Sundered Realm. It resonates with a raw, untamed magic. If the Veil were to completely dissipate in this area, such energies would flood into our world, with catastrophic consequences. Your ancestors' role was to prevent such a cataclysm."

Kael's mental voice was urgent. "The whispers are growing louder, Elara. The entities are testing the boundaries. They sense the potential for breach. They are drawn by the very essence of your lineage, a scent they have long craved."

Elara looked at the locket, then at Borin and Kael. The path ahead was daunting, shrouded in mystery and fraught with peril. But for the first time, she understood the true scope of what lay before her. It was not just about mastering runes or defending herself; it was about understanding and protecting the delicate balance between worlds, a balance that her own bloodline had been sworn to uphold. The Sundered Realm was no longer a myth; it was a tangible reality, and her connection to it was undeniable. The Veil between worlds was not just a concept; it was a battlefield, and she was now its newest recruit. The responsibility settled upon her shoulders, heavy but galvanizing. The whispers were not just a threat; they were a call to arms. And she would answer.

Kael shifted, his lupine form exuding an aura of quiet vigilance that spoke of eons spent in watchfulness. Elara felt a subtle shift in the air, as if the very stones of Borin's workshop vibrated with a deeper resonance. The whispers, once a disquieting murmur, now seemed to coalesce into a symphony of warning, a testament to the thinning Veil and the growing proximity of... *others.*

"Guardians of the Threshold," Kael's mental voice echoed, the words resonating with a profound weight. "It is a title bestowed upon those who stand between the worlds. My kind, the Lycanthrope of the Elder Peaks, have long been intertwined with the Weavers. We are watchers, protectors, and sometimes, conduits."

Elara's gaze flickered to Kael, his golden eyes burning with an ancient wisdom that belied his animal form. He was more than just a companion; he was a link to a forgotten past, a living testament to the secrets she was only beginning to uncover. Borin, his hands still, observed the exchange with a placid intensity, his presence a grounding force amidst the unfolding revelations.

"Your parents," Kael continued, his mental voice laced with a sorrow that Elara felt as a tangible ache in her own heart, "they were among the most capable Guardians I have ever known. Their understanding of the Veil, of its intricacies and its vulnerabilities, was unparalleled. They walked the liminal spaces, Elara, not as trespassers, but as stewards. Their lives were a testament to the sacred trust placed upon your bloodline."

He paused, and Elara sensed a heavy unspoken burden settling upon him. "Their end," Kael's voice became a low, guttural growl that seemed to vibrate through the very air, "was a consequence of that stewardship. The forces that sought to tear down the Veil are not new. They are ancient, relentless, and they hunger for the raw power that flows between realms. Your parents stood against them, not with the clatter of steel, but with the intricate weave of arcane energy, with the very essence of their being."

Elara's breath caught in her throat. The vague fear that had clung to her since her parents' disappearance now solidified into a horrifying certainty. They had not simply vanished; they had fought, and likely fallen, in a battle that raged in the unseen spaces, a battle for the very fabric of existence. The locket around her neck, warm against her skin, suddenly felt like a tangible piece of that struggle, a legacy passed down from those who had paid the ultimate price.

"The order of the Guardians," Borin interjected, his voice a low rumble that complemented Kael's, "is not something born of decree. It is a calling, a responsibility etched into the souls of those who bear the mark of the Weavers. They are the linchpins, Elara, the ones who anchor the Veil, who mend its tears, and who, when necessary, guide lost souls – or unwelcome ones – back to their proper places."

He gestured to a collection of intricately carved stones scattered across his workbench, each one humming with a latent energy. "Your ancestors did not simply *create* the Veil; they *were* the Veil, in a sense. Their magic was so intrinsically linked to its structure that they could shape and mold it with their intent. They understood the delicate balance, the ebb and flow of primal forces. This understanding is now dormant within you, a seed waiting to be nurtured."

Kael's mental presence pulsed with a gentle encouragement. "My purpose, child, is to help you awaken that seed. Your parents entrusted me with their knowledge, with their hopes for your future. They knew that the burden they carried would one day fall to you. They foresaw the continued threats to the Veil, the escalating aggression of the entities that dwell in the shadowed chasms between worlds. I am here to ensure that you are not merely a target, but a defender."

He looked at Elara, his golden gaze holding a depth of understanding that transcended words. "The whispers, Elara, are not merely a manifestation of your burgeoning power. They are probes, testing the integrity of the Veil, sensing its weaknesses. And they are drawn to you, a beacon of the Weaver bloodline. Your parents recognized this threat, and they prepared. They imbued the locket, not just with their lineage, but with a portion of their vigilance, their knowledge of the enemy, and their unyielding resolve."

Elara clutched the locket, it's cool metal a stark contrast to the warmth of her racing heart. She had always felt a sense of longing, a feeling of being incomplete, as if a vital part of her had been lost with her parents. Now, she understood. That missing piece was not just a familial connection; it was the legacy of guardianship, the profound responsibility that had defined their lives and, it seemed, was destined to define hers.

"The entities," Kael continued, his voice a low murmur that seemed to emanate from the very earth beneath them, "are drawn to raw magical energy. Our world, filled with the vibrant life force of its inhabitants, is a tempting feast. The Sundered Realm, a place of untamed creation, offers even greater sustenance. The Veil is the buffer, the protective membrane that prevents the uncontrolled influx of such power, and the subsequent devastation of both realms."

He shifted his weight, his muscles coiling beneath his fur. "Your parents understood that maintaining the Veil was not a passive act. It required constant vigilance, an active defense. They would patrol the thinning places, reinforce the weakened sections, and sometimes, confront those who sought to exploit the breaches. Their training was rigorous, their dedication absolute. And it is that same rigor, that same dedication, that I will impart to you."

Borin picked up a small, unadorned wooden box from a shelf, his movements precise and deliberate. He opened it to reveal a collection of smooth, dark stones, each no larger than a thumbnail. "These are Echo Stones," he explained, his voice resonating with a quiet authority. "Each one is attuned to a specific resonance within the Veil. Your parents used them to track the ebb and flow of energies, to identify areas of instability. They are tools, Elara, but tools that require a discerning hand and a deep understanding of the currents they represent."

He offered a stone to Elara. As her fingers brushed against its surface, a faint tremor ran through her. It was like touching a distant memory, a faint echo of something vast and powerful. "When the Veil thins significantly," Borin continued, "these stones will vibrate, their resonance intensifying. They will guide you, not just to the thinning places, but to the nature of the disruption. Some breaches are caused by natural fluctuations in magical energy; others are the deliberate work of malevolent entities."

Kael's mental voice sharpened. "The entities you have sensed, the whispers you have heard, are the vanguard. They are testing the boundaries, seeking vulnerabilities. Your awakening has made you a more prominent signal, a more tempting target. They sense the potential for a breach, and they are drawn to the possibility of exploiting it through you."

He met Elara's gaze, his eyes a piercing golden light. "Your parents believed that the Veil was not merely a barrier, but a sacred covenant between realms. A testament to the understanding that each world had its place, its purpose, its right to exist without being consumed by the other. They died defending that covenant. And now, that same duty falls to you."

Elara felt a surge of adrenaline, a potent mix of fear and resolve. The weight of her lineage, the legacy of her parents, settled upon her shoulders. It was a terrifying prospect, but also, in a strange way, a comforting one. She was not alone in this; she had Kael, a Guardian whose loyalty and wisdom were as ancient as the mountains, and Borin, a master craftsman who understood the fundamental forces that shaped reality.

"The Guardians," Kael explained, his voice a low rumble of ancient knowledge, "are more than just protectors. We are also guides. When individuals within this world begin to exhibit the latent abilities that connect them to the Sundered Realm, it is our duty to find them, to understand the nature of their awakening, and to ensure that their power is not a danger to themselves or to the balance of the Veil."

He nudged Elara's hand with his snout, a gesture of reassurance that resonated with a profound understanding. "Your parents understood this role intimately. They trained diligently, not just in the weaving of arcane energies, but in the subtle art of diplomacy between realms. They knew that not all entities from the Sundered Realm were inherently hostile. Some were simply lost, displaced, or seeking refuge. Their task was to discern, to guide, and to protect."

Borin held up one of the carved stones, turning it in his calloused fingers. "This stone," he said, "is attuned to the general resonance of the Veil. But your parents created specialized stones, attuned to specific threats, specific breaches. They were like a specialized toolkit, each designed for a particular challenge. They understood that the Veil was not a monolithic entity, but a complex tapestry, with threads that could be frayed, weakened, or even deliberately severed."

Kael's mental voice grew serious. "The entities that haunt the edges of the Veil are driven by hunger. They crave the raw, vibrant energies of your world, the life force that sustains its inhabitants. They see the Veil as a dam holding back an inexhaustible river, and they seek to break it, to flood our reality with their insatiable need. Your parents fought to reinforce that dam, to mend the cracks before they became fissures."

Elara looked at the locket, then at the stones in Borin's hand, and finally at Kael. The pieces were beginning to fall into place, forming a picture far grander and more terrifying than she could have ever imagined. Her parents' deaths, her own awakening, the whispers – they were all threads in a much larger tapestry, a cosmic struggle for the fate of existence itself.

"The order," Kael continued, his voice a low thrum of ancient lore, "is not bound by blood alone, but by a shared understanding of the delicate balance. We are the custodians of that balance, the silent watchers who ensure that the currents of magic do not overwhelm the mundane, and that the vitality of life is not leached away by forces that do not understand its value. Your parents were exemplary in this regard, their lives a beacon of dedication."

He met Elara's gaze, his golden eyes reflecting the dim light of Borin's workshop. "They entrusted me with ensuring that their legacy would continue. That you, Elara, would be prepared. The path you are now on is not one of your choosing, but it is a path woven into the very fabric of your being. The blood of the Weavers carries with it not only the power to shape reality, but the responsibility to protect it."

Borin nodded, his expression one of solemn understanding. "The runes you have learned, Elara, are not merely symbols. They are the fundamental building blocks of existence, the very threads with which the Veil was woven. Your ancestors understood this on a primal level. They could manipulate these threads, reinforce them, or even unravel them with their will. Your training is to reawaken that innate understanding, to allow you to commune with the Veil itself."

He picked up another stone, this one pulsing with a faint, almost imperceptible warmth. "This stone," Borin explained, "is a resonance amplifier. When placed near a thinning place, it will amplify the Veil's natural emanations, making it easier to perceive the subtle shifts and anomalies. Your parents used these extensively, charting the Veil's pulse, much like a healer would monitor a patient's heartbeat."

Kael's mental voice was tinged with a sense of urgency. "The entities are growing bolder, Elara. The whispers are no longer mere probes; they are invitations, attempts to lure you into compromising situations, to exploit your nascent abilities before you fully understand them. They sense your connection to the Weaver bloodline, and they see you as a potential key to unlocking the Veil completely."

Elara ran a finger over the smooth surface of the locket. It felt heavier now, laden with the weight of her parents' sacrifice and the responsibility that was now hers. The whispers, once a source of fear, now seemed to carry a different meaning. They were not just the voices of malevolent entities; they were also the echoes of her ancestors, a silent plea to uphold the ancient duty.

"The Sundered Realm," Kael continued, his voice a low rumble of ancient sorrow and fierce protectiveness, "is a place of immense power, but also of immense fragility. It is a realm of pure creation, where energies coalesce and dissipate with an almost frightening speed. Your ancestors, the Elder Weavers, understood this duality. They were the architects of balance, the ones who ensured that the raw power of the Sundered Realm did not overwhelm the more structured reality of this world."

He let out a low sigh, a sound of weariness that spoke of countless vigils. "Your parents were the latest in a long line of Guardians. They dedicated their lives to this work, to the constant vigilance required to maintain the integrity of the Veil. They understood the cost, the isolation, the constant threat of forces that would see both worlds consumed. They fought not just with magic, but with an unwavering resolve, a profound understanding of the stakes."

Borin carefully placed the Echo Stones back into their wooden box. "The path of a Guardian is not an easy one, Elara. It is a path of sacrifice, of constant vigilance, and often, of profound loneliness. But it is also a path of immense purpose. You carry the blood of those who shaped reality, who stood between worlds and protected the fragile peace. Your parents understood this, and they prepared you, even before you were aware of it."

Kael nudged Elara's hand again, a silent reassurance that bridged the gap between their species, between worlds. "You are a Weaver, Elara. A descendant of those who commanded the threads of existence. The Veil needs its guardians, now more than ever. The whispers are not just a warning; they are a call to action. And I, along with Borin, will stand with you as you answer it."

The weight on Elara's shoulders remained, but it was no longer just a burden. It was also a source of strength, a tangible connection to her past and a clear indication of her future. The locket pulsed with a faint warmth against her skin, a promise of the knowledge and power that lay dormant within her, waiting to be awakened. The Guardians of the Threshold, a lineage whispered through the ages, now had a new recruit, ready to face the echoes of a sundered realm.

The weight of Kael's words settled upon Elara like a shroud woven from ancient starlight and forgotten sorrow. She clutched the locket, its familiar coolness now a stark counterpoint to the sudden heat that bloomed within her chest. It was more than a relic, more than a symbol of her lineage; it was a nexus, a key, a whisper from a past that was both hers and utterly alien. The meditation Kael had proposed, a deep plunge into the swirling currents of her own latent power, felt less like an option and more like an imperative.

"Meditate, Elara," Kael's mental voice resonated, a low, steady hum against the rising tide of her apprehension. "Focus on the locket. Let its presence anchor you. Do not fight the whispers, but listen. They are fragmented, yes, but within their disjointed echoes lie the threads of your inheritance."

Borin, with a quiet efficiency, dimmed the lanterns in his workshop, casting long, dancing shadows that seemed to writhe with unspoken stories. The air grew heavy, charged with a palpable anticipation. Elara settled onto a cushion, the rough weave a grounding sensation against her bare legs. She closed her eyes, the image of the locket imprinted behind her eyelids. It was a simple silver oval, etched with intricate, swirling patterns that seemed to shift and reform the longer she looked. Her parents' faces, smiling, loving, flashed briefly, then dissolved into the shimmering haze.

133

"Breathe," Kael's voice guided, a gentle current in the turbulent waters of her mind. "Inhale the present. Exhale the doubt. The locket is a gateway, Elara. Not just to the Veil, but to the essence of those who came before. Your parents poured their final moments, their knowledge, their very spirits into its core. It is a chronicle, a living testament."

She focused on the warmth radiating from the silver against her skin. It was a comforting heat, like a hearth fire on a cold night, but beneath it, a subtle thrumming began. It was a faint vibration at first, barely perceptible, like the distant heartbeat of a sleeping titan. The whispers, which had been a disquieting murmur at the edges of her awareness, now seemed to draw closer, coalescing around this central pulse. They were no longer chaotic; they were layered, interwoven, like the delicate strands of a tapestry.

As she delved deeper, letting the meditation guide her, the locket's thrumming intensified. The swirling patterns on its surface seemed to come alive, projecting faint, ethereal images into the darkness behind her eyes. A woman's hand, her mother's, reached out, tracing the same patterns on a sun-drenched hillside. The scent of wild herbs, sharp and sweet, filled Elara's senses, a phantom aroma that made her breath catch. Then, a man's voice, her father's, boomed with laughter, the sound echoing from a windswept cliff. He held a glowing shard of crystal, its light pulsing in time with the locket.

"They were fighting," Kael's voice cut through the reverie, sharp with a sorrow Elara felt as if it were her own. "Not just defending. They were trying to *seal* something. A tear in the Veil, larger than any I have witnessed in centuries. The energies that poured through... they were raw, primal, the very essence of unmaking."

The images shifted, growing more frantic. A vortex of shimmering, impossible colors tore through a landscape that was both familiar and terrifyingly distorted. Buildings twisted and contorted, the very laws of physics seemingly unraveling. Her parents stood at the precipice of this chaos, their forms wreathed in arcs of protective light, their faces etched with grim determination. Elara saw her mother weaving intricate sigils in the air, the patterns mirroring those on the locket. Her father hurled bolts of pure energy, each one a desperate plea for order.

"The Sundered Realm," Elara whispered, the words foreign yet resonating deep within her soul.

"Indeed," Kael confirmed, his mental voice laced with a profound sadness. "A place of chaotic creation, where form and function are fluid. Your ancestors, the Elder Weavers, understood its volatile nature. They built the Veil as a bulwark, a containment field to prevent its untamed energies from spilling into your world. But the Sundered Realm is not static. It churns, it grows, and sometimes, it reaches out."

The visions intensified. Elara saw her parents desperately channeling their combined might into the locket, a final, agonizing act of transference. It was not just their power they imbued, but their memories, their experiences, their very consciousness, fragmented and scattered, but preserved. The locket became their final testament, a way to communicate what they could no longer say, to show what they could no longer live to explain.

"They knew they couldn't win," Elara murmured, a cold dread seeping into her bones. "They knew they were going to fall."

"They chose to fall," Kael corrected, his voice firm, devoid of judgment. "They chose to protect. The tear they fought to mend was not an accident. It was a deliberate breach, orchestrated by entities from the Sundered Realm who sought to consume your world. Your parents sacrificed themselves to ensure that the Veil held, even if only for a time. And they entrusted this locket, this repository of their struggle, to you."

135

Elara felt a profound connection to the woman in the visions, her mother. She saw her fierce love, her unwavering resolve, her deep sorrow for the daughter she would never see grow up. She understood the weight of her father's burden, the immense responsibility he carried, the desperate hope that their sacrifice would not be in vain. These were not just fleeting images; they were visceral experiences, emotions that washed over her in waves, leaving her breathless and profoundly altered.

"The locket... It's not just a key to the Veil," Elara realized aloud, her voice trembling. "It's... It's them. Pieces of them. Their knowledge. Their fight."

"Precisely," Kael confirmed. "Each memory, each fragment of knowledge, is a shard of truth. When you attune yourself to it, you are essentially communing with their spirits, accessing the echoes of their lives. It is how they will guide you, Elara. How will they teach you what you need to know to continue their work?"

The visions began to coalesce around a single, cataclysmic event. A blinding white light erupted from the center of the tearing Veil, a force so immense it seemed to rip reality itself asunder. Elara felt a searing pain, a desperate surge of power, and then... nothing. Darkness. A profound, chilling void that swallowed all sensation. She understood then that this was the moment of their disappearance, the catastrophic Sundering that had fractured their realm and claimed their lives.

"The Sundering," Borin's voice, usually so steady, held a note of awe and trepidation. "It is said that the Veil was never truly the same after that day. The fabric was weakened, scarred. This locket is a living chronicle of that scar, a testament to the forces that inflicted it."

As Elara emerged from the meditation, the workshop felt both the same and irrevocably different. The air, once merely charged, now hummed with the residual energy of the visions. The locket felt warm against her skin, no longer just a piece of metal, but a conduit, a direct link to her parents and to the epic struggle they had waged.

"They are within you, Elara," Kael's mental voice resonated, soft now, filled with a deep respect. "Their strength, their knowledge, their determination. The locket is the key to unlocking that inheritance. But it is not a passive gift. It requires understanding, discipline, and a willingness to embrace the truth of your lineage."

He looked at her, his golden eyes reflecting a wisdom that spanned millennia. "The memories you saw are fragmented, incomplete. Your parents' essence was scattered, dispersed in the Sundering. But with each meditation, with each attunement, you will piece together more of the puzzle. You will learn of their techniques, their strategies, and their understanding of the entities that threaten the Veil. You will learn what they learned, in the crucible of their final moments."

Elara touched the locket again, the cool silver a familiar comfort. It was no longer just a beautiful heirloom. It was a library of her past, a map to her future, and a testament to the sacrifices of two people she had barely known, but whose courage now echoed within her own soul. The whispers were still there, but they no longer felt like a threat. They felt like a conversation, a dialogue across time, guided by the spirits of her parents, channeled through the very locket that now rested against her heart. The path ahead was daunting, paved with the echoes of a sundered realm, but for the first time, Elara felt a flicker of true understanding, a nascent sense of purpose. She was not merely a descendant of the Weavers; she was a continuation of their legacy, a living archive of their struggle, armed with the echoes of their lives. The locket was not just a tool; it was a living testament, a silent promise that their fight, their knowledge, and their love would endure. It was the most profound inheritance imaginable, a burden and a gift intertwined, whispering of the immense responsibility that now rested upon her young shoulders. She understood that her journey was not about discovering what the locket could do, but about what it would allow her to *become*, shaped by the very essence of her lost parents. The fragments of memory were not just stories; they were lessons, etched into the very fabric of the locket, waiting for her to decipher them, to absorb them, and ultimately, to wield them. The echoes of the Sundered Realm were now her own, a symphony of power and peril that would guide her steps.

The whispers, once ethereal echoes, began to coalesce into a more discernible narrative. They spoke of a presence, a profound darkness that predated even the Sundering, a malevolence that festered in the interstitial spaces between realities. This was not a force of nature, nor a chaotic surge of untamed energy. This was a will, ancient and terrible, a consciousness driven by an insatiable hunger for dominion. Elara, with each deepening attunement to the locket, felt the icy tendrils of this ancient dread reach for her, a psychic chill that threatened to extinguish the nascent embers of her own power.

She saw flashes of its influence, subtle at first, then growing in magnitude. It was the unseen hand that nudged events towards discord, the subtle corruption that frayed the edges of peace. The Elder Weavers, the architects of the Veil, had known of this threat. Their chronicles, fragmented within the locket, spoke of a primeval entity, a being they had only dared to name in hushed tones: the Shadow Lord. He was not of the Sundered Realm, nor of Elara's world, but a perversion of both, a being who drew sustenance from the very fabric of existence, twisting it to his own bleak design.

Her parents' memories, when they touched upon him, were tinged with a desperate urgency. They depicted not a direct confrontation, but a desperate struggle to contain his machinations. He was the architect of the breach, the one who had deliberately weakened the Veil, not to unleash the Sundered Realm's chaos, but to sow the seeds of his own dominion. The catastrophic events that had fractured their world and led to their sacrifice were not an accident of cosmic alignment, but a calculated maneuver by this ancient foe.

He sought to extinguish all light, all hope, all life, and plunge existence into an eternal, suffocating night.

Elara witnessed the immense effort her parents had expended, not just in fighting the chaotic energies but in actively combating the Shadow Lord's influence. They had built wards, woven enchantments, and performed rituals designed to push back his encroaching darkness. The locket, she now understood, was not merely a repository of their final moments; it was also a chronicle of their knowledge regarding this ancient enemy. It held the keys to understanding his nature, his weaknesses, and the subtle ways he manipulated the fabric of reality.

The visions grew more vivid, more terrifying. She saw Elara's mother tracing intricate patterns in the air, not of protection, but of *binding*. Her father, his face etched with a weariness that transcended physical exhaustion, was channeling raw, volatile energies, not to destroy, but to *seal*. They were fighting a losing battle, not against an overwhelming physical force, but against a pervasive, insidious corruption that sought to infect everything it touched. The Shadow Lord was a master manipulator, a weaver of despair, who exploited fear and doubt like a skilled artisan.

"He feeds on the imbalance," Kael's voice echoed, softer now, as if the shared understanding of this ancient evil had brought a somber reverence to his tone. "The Sundered Realm is a place of extreme duality, of creation and unmaking. The Shadow Lord exploits this, amplifying the unmaking, twisting creation into monstrous forms. He sought to do the same to your world, Elara. To turn its light into shadow, its order into chaos, its life into a barren wasteland under his eternal reign."

The locket pulsed with a cold energy as Elara absorbed the weight of this revelation. Her parents had not just died defending their world; they had died fighting an ancient, intelligent evil that had orchestrated their world's sundering. The Breach, the event that had created the Sundered Realm and torn Elara's family apart, was a weapon wielded by the Shadow Lord. He had seen the Veil not as a barrier to be respected, but as a dam waiting to be broken, releasing a flood of despair that would engulf all.

The fragmented memories showed her glimpses of his true form, or rather, the absence of it. He was a swirling vortex of shadow, a void that seemed to absorb all light and sound. There were no features, no discernible shape, only an immense, palpable aura of malevolence that promised annihilation. Yet, within this terrifying void, there were whispers of intelligence, of cunning, of an ancient, cold ambition that chilled Elara to the bone. He was not a creature of instinct, but of purpose, and that purpose was the utter eradication of all that was good and vibrant.

"He is not a physical entity in the way we understand it," Kael explained, his mental presence a steadying force against the encroaching dread. "He is a manifestation of the antithesis of existence. A predator that thrives on entropy. Your parents understood this. They knew that brute force would not suffice. They had to counter his darkness with a different kind of light, a light that understood and contained, rather than merely destroyed."

Elara saw her parents working in tandem, their powers merging, creating a complex weave of energy that seemed to push back against an unseen tide. It was a dance of desperate preservation, a ritual of defiance against an enemy who sought to unravel the very threads of reality. The locket, she realized, was a culmination of this fight, a final repository of their struggle and their knowledge, a weapon of sorts, imbued with their essence and their understanding of the Shadow Lord.

The memory fragments continued to unfold, revealing more about the nature of the Shadow Lord's influence. He was a master of corruption, not just of realms, but of individuals. He whispered temptations, preyed on insecurities, and amplified negative emotions, turning hope into despair, love into hatred, and courage into fear. He was a parasite that fed on the darkness within all living things, seeking to expand his dominion by twisting and corrupting the light.

"He is patient," Kael warned, his voice somber. "His influence may have been curtailed by your parents' sacrifice, but it has not been eradicated. The Veil is weakened, Elara. The breach, though sealed, has left scars. And through these scars, his whispers still reach out. He will seek any weakness, any flicker of doubt, to reassert his control. He is the shadow that hunts the light, and you, Elara, are now a beacon."

Elara felt the truth of Kael's words resonate within her. The Shadow Lord was not a distant, abstract threat. He was an active force, a lingering darkness that sought to exploit the very vulnerabilities that the Sundering had created. The fragmented memories were not just a history lesson; they were a warning. Her parents had fought him with everything they had, and their struggle was now her own. The locket, once a symbol of her lost family, was now a testament to their fight against this ancient evil, and a tool that would allow her to continue it.

She saw the terrifying moment when the Shadow Lord's influence had reached its zenith, when the breach had widened, and the raw, unmaking energies of the Sundered Realm had begun to spill forth. It was not a mindless cataclysm, but a deliberate act, orchestrated by the Shadow Lord to destabilize both realms and create an opening for his own dominion. Her parents had thrown themselves into the heart of this maelstrom, not to conquer, but to contain, to protect, to ensure that his victory would not be absolute.

The visions shifted, showing her the Shadow Lord's attempts to corrupt her parents, to twist their noble intentions into instruments of his own dark will. He had offered them power, dominion, a chance to restore their world, but at a terrible price. The memories showed their unwavering refusal, their commitment to a higher ideal, their ultimate sacrifice born not of defeat, but of an unyielding defiance. They had chosen oblivion over corruption, self-annihilation over servitude to the darkness.

"They understood that his power was not of this world, and that it could not be defeated by the conventional means of ours," Kael elaborated, his voice filled with a profound respect for her parents' resolve. "They had to use a different kind of magic, a magic that understood the fundamental nature of his being, a magic that could bind and contain rather than simply destroy. The locket is imbued with that knowledge, Elara. It is a testament to their understanding, and a legacy of their courage."

As Elara delved deeper into the locket's memories, she began to piece together a clearer picture of the Shadow Lord's ultimate goal. He did not merely seek to conquer; he sought to unmake. He craved an existence devoid of light, of joy, of life itself. The Sundered Realm, with its chaotic energies and its fractured reality, was a breeding ground for his influence, a perfect canvas upon which to paint his masterpiece of despair. And his ultimate target was Elara's world, a realm of vibrant life and ordered existence, the antithesis of everything he represented.

The weight of this knowledge pressed down on her, a crushing realization of the immensity of the threat. Her parents had fought a valiant battle, but they had not won. They had merely delayed the inevitable, containing the Shadow Lord's influence and preventing him from achieving his ultimate goal. The Veil, though scarred, still held, but it was a fragile barrier, and the Shadow Lord was a persistent enemy, patient and cunning, waiting for an opportunity to strike again.

"He is still out there, Elara." Kael's voice was a grave pronouncement, resonating with the unspoken truth of their predicament. "His influence may be muted, but it has not vanished. The echoes of his malevolence still linger in the fractured spaces. He will be watching, waiting for any sign of weakness, any opportunity to breach the Veil once more. Your parents' sacrifice bought time, but it did not secure a lasting peace. That, Elara, is the task that now falls to you."

The fragmented memories of the locket painted a grim but illuminating picture. The Shadow Lord was not a simple villain, but a cosmic force of destruction, an ancient evil that had been a thorn in the side of creation since time immemorial. Her parents had faced him in a desperate struggle, a battle that had cost them everything, but which had preserved the hope for future generations. And now, that hope rested with Elara, armed with the fragmented knowledge of her ancestors and the ever-present whispers of the Shadow Lord's enduring threat. The locket, a conduit to her past, was now her most potent weapon against the encroaching darkness, a constant reminder of the stakes involved in the ongoing war between light and shadow.

The air in the chamber grew heavy, thick with an unspoken dread that coiled around Elara like a serpent. Kael's words, delivered with a somber gravitas, painted a picture of cosmic fragility. The Veil, that ethereal bulwark separating worlds, was not an immutable force, but a dynamic membrane, susceptible to the ravages of time and the lingering malevolence of forces like the Shadow Lord. Each whispered echo Elara had deciphered from the locket, each fragment of her parents' desperate struggle, served as a testament to its enduring importance, and now, its alarming vulnerability.

"The Veil is not merely a physical barrier," Kael explained, his mental voice a low rumble that vibrated within Elara's very bones. "It is woven from the very essence of stability, the inherent order that prevents the raw, untamed energies of the cosmos from bleeding into one another. Think of it as a tapestry, Elara, meticulously crafted by the Elder Weavers. But time, and the insidious influence of beings like the Shadow Lord, are like a relentless moth, gnawing at its threads, weakening its structure."

Elara absorbed his words, her mind replaying the fragmented visions. She saw not just the chaotic surge of the Sundered Realm, but the subtle, deliberate manipulations of the Shadow Lord, seeking any fracture, any weakness, to exploit. His presence, even when contained, was like a slow poison seeping into the foundations of reality.

"The Shadow Lord's defeat was not absolute," Kael continued, his tone deepening with concern. "He was banished, yes, his power temporarily curtailed. But his essence, his malevolence, it lingers. It pollutes the interstitial spaces, the cracks in the Veil that were widened during the Sundering. And with each passing era, these scars fester, the weakened points of the Veil grow more pronounced. The energies of the Sundered Realm, already volatile, find it easier to seep through, to whisper their chaos into our world."

He paused, allowing the weight of his revelation to settle. "This weakening is not merely a passive decay, Elara. It is an invitation. An invitation for the realms to converge. Imagine two oceans, separated by a flimsy dam. The dam is weakening, and the pressure is building. Eventually, the dam will break, and the waters will merge, leading to unimaginable upheaval. This is the impending convergence Kael had spoken of, a catastrophic event where the boundaries between our reality and the Sundered Realm, and perhaps even other shadowed planes touched by the Shadow Lord's influence, could blur and eventually dissolve."

Elara's breath hitched. The idea was terrifying, a cosmic tidal wave of destruction. Her parents' sacrifice, the containment they had so desperately enacted, had been a temporary measure, a patching of the dam, not a rebuilding. The Shadow Lord's lingering tendrils, like unseen currents, had continued to erode its foundations.

"You asked why your awakening, why the locket's resonance, has intensified now," Kael said, his voice laced with a growing urgency. "It is no coincidence. Your awakening is intrinsically linked to this impending convergence. The heightened sensitivity you feel, the influx of knowledge, it is the Veil itself reacting to the growing instability. And you, Elara, you are at the epicenter of this disturbance."

He projected an image into her mind, a swirling vortex of light and shadow, representing the Veil. At its heart, a delicate, pulsating energy – Elara. Around her, tendrils of darkness, the Shadow Lord's residual influence, and streams of chaotic, untamed energy from the Sundered Realm, all pressing inwards, converging on her.

"The convergence is not merely an event; it is a process," Kael elaborated. "And your unique connection to the locket, your nascent abilities, they are a crucial factor in this process. You are not merely an observer, Elara. You are a catalyst. You possess the potential to either reinforce the Veil, to mend the shattered tapestry, or, if your power is insufficient, if your will falters, you could inadvertently become the conduit through which the darkness seeps, allowing the realms to merge in a cataclysm of untold proportions."

The burden of his words settled upon her, a weight heavier than any physical object. Her parents had fought to prevent this very outcome. Their final act, their ultimate sacrifice, had been to preserve the integrity of the Veil, to buy time for a future when this threat could be definitively dealt with. And now, that future had arrived, and the responsibility rested squarely on her shoulders.

"Your parents understood the delicate balance," Kael continued, his voice a soothing balm against the rising tide of her apprehension. "They knew that brute force alone would not suffice against the Shadow Lord. His power was rooted in the antithesis of existence, a force that thrived on entropy and despair. To combat him, they needed to understand not just his malice but the very fabric of reality he sought to unravel. The locket contains not only their memories, but their understanding of the Veil, its construction, its vulnerabilities, and the ancient magics used to sustain it."

Elara touched the locket hanging around her neck. It felt warmer now, almost alive, a tangible link to her parents' wisdom and their desperate struggle. The fragmented visions within it were no longer just historical records; they were a training manual, a guide to the esoteric knowledge required to mend what had been broken.

"The convergence is not a single, explosive event," Kael clarified. "It is a gradual intertwining. The boundaries will thin. Places where the Veil is weakest will become… porous. Portals might flicker into existence, not grand, obvious gates, but subtle tears through which creatures and energies can pass. Memories of the Sundered Realm might bleed into our own, causing confusion, madness, and a growing sense of unease. Your world's inherent order will be tested, its light dimmed by the encroaching shadows."

He showed her glimpses of what this might look like. A forest where the trees twisted into unnatural, skeletal shapes, their leaves replaced by withered husks. A sky where the sun flickered, casting an eerie, dualistic light, as if two suns, one vibrant and the other deathly pale, were struggling for dominance. Whispers on the wind that sounded like the tormented cries of forgotten souls. The mundane world would begin to fray at the edges, succumbing to a creeping, existential dread.

"The Shadow Lord's influence is subtle," Kael warned. "He doesn't always manifest as a direct assault. He amplifies existing fears, sows discord, and exploits weaknesses. With the Veil thinning, his whispers will grow louder, his insidious suggestions more potent. He will feed on the fear generated by the convergence, using it to further destabilize the boundaries and hasten the merging of realms. He wants to plunge everything into his favored state: oblivion, a void where only he can exist."

Elara clenched her fists, the images searing themselves into her mind. The thought of her world succumbing to such a fate, of the beauty and life she knew being extinguished, fueled a nascent fire within her. This was not just about understanding her parents' legacy; it was about safeguarding everything they had died to protect.

"Your awakening is not a random surge of power," Kael reiterated, emphasizing the critical nature of her role. "It is a response. The Veil, sensing its own potential collapse, is reaching out. It is amplifying your connection to the locket, to the echoes of your parents' knowledge, because it needs you. It needs someone who can understand the intricate weave of reality, someone who can counter the Shadow Lord's unraveling."

He projected another vision, this time of her parents, their forms shimmering with ethereal light, working in tandem. They were not fighting a tangible enemy, but weaving complex patterns of energy, not to destroy, but to reinforce, to mend. Their hands moved with a fluid grace, their movements echoing the ancient rhythms of creation. The locket, he indicated, was a focal point of their efforts, a repository of that specific, delicate magic.

"The magic your parents employed was not the magic of brute force, of raw elemental power," Kael explained. "It was the magic of understanding, of intricate knowledge. It was the art of mending, of reinforcing the fabric of existence. They learned this art from the Elder Weavers, and they poured their understanding and their very essence into the locket. It is a key, Elara, a repository of the knowledge you will need to seal the Veil, to push back against the convergence."

The sheer immensity of the task was daunting. She was a young woman, still grappling with the echoes of a fragmented past, suddenly thrust into a cosmic struggle for existence. But as she looked at the locket, felt its warmth against her skin, she felt a flicker of defiance ignite within her. Her parents had not given up. They had fought with every fiber of their being, and their fight had not been in vain. They had left her with the tools, the knowledge, and most importantly, the will to continue their work.

"The convergence is not merely about the Sundered Realm," Kael added, a new layer of complexity to his warning. "The Shadow Lord is a master of exploitation. He seeks to create as many points of entry as possible. The weakened Veil, exacerbated by the chaos of the Sundering, is a prime target. He will exploit any rift, any tear, to further his agenda of unmaking. The convergence might manifest in unexpected ways, in places you least suspect. The boundaries between our world and others, places that have long been dormant, could stir once more."

Elara recalled fragments from the locket – whispers of ancient pacts, of realms forgotten, of entities that slumbered in the deep cosmic currents. Was the Shadow Lord's influence reaching out to these forgotten places as well, seeking to awaken them and draw them into the brewing storm? The possibilities were endless, and each one painted a more terrifying picture of the unfolding crisis.

"Your parents' goal was to seal the Veil, not just against the Sundered Realm, but against any manifestation of the Shadow Lord's influence," Kael stated. "They understood that his darkness was not confined to one dimension. It was a pervasive entity, capable of infecting any realm that strayed from the path of light and order. The locket holds the key to understanding that sealing process, not just as a barrier, but as a restoration of balance."

He projected another set of fragmented images, showing Elara's parents performing complex rituals, their hands tracing patterns in the air that mirrored the intricate geometries of the Veil itself. They were not merely closing a door; they were reweaving the very fabric of reality, strengthening its integrity, pushing back against the encroaching void. The locket pulsed with a faint light in these visions, a symbol of their concentrated effort, their borrowed strength.

"Your awakening is the locket's response to the growing instability," Kael reiterated, his voice firm. "It is calling to you, Elara, because it recognizes your lineage, your potential, and the critical juncture in time. You are the living embodiment of the balance your parents fought to preserve. The convergence is the ultimate test of that balance. Your path forward will involve understanding and mastering the knowledge within the locket, learning to harness its power, and ultimately, using it to reinforce the Veil, to prevent the Shadow Lord from achieving his catastrophic objective."

The path ahead seemed impossibly steep, fraught with peril and uncertainty. But as Elara stood in the hushed chamber, the weight of the locket a constant, reassuring presence against her chest, she felt a resolve hardening within her. Her parents had faced the abyss and refused to yield. They had sacrificed everything to give her a chance. Now, it was her turn to honor their legacy, to face the encroaching darkness, and to fight for the light. The impending convergence was not just a harbinger of destruction; it was a call to arms, and she would answer.

CHAPTER 5:

EMBRACING THE LEGACY

The journey to the celestial citadel was a descent into a world woven from mist and memory. Kael's presence, a luminous thread in Elara's mind, guided her steps through landscapes that shifted and warped with the capricious nature of forgotten magic. The air grew colder, carrying with it the scent of damp earth and the faint, metallic tang of ozone, a telltale sign of frayed magical energies. The world Elara had known, with its familiar flora and fauna, gradually receded, replaced by a twilight realm where the very shadows seemed to possess a sentience. Twisted trees, their bark like petrified bone, clawed at a sky perpetually veiled in pearlescent clouds. Strange, phosphorescent fungi pulsed with a soft, internal light, casting ethereal glows that did little to dispel the pervasive gloom.

As they drew closer, the whispers, once confined to the locket and Kael's mental voice, began to manifest in the environment itself. They were not words, not in any language Elara understood, but rather a tapestry of emotions, impressions, and fleeting images that brushed against her mind like cobwebs. Fear, longing, a profound sense of loss, and an almost unbearable weight of ancient duty – these were the textures of the whispers, the echoes of the citadel's past. They spoke of the constant struggle to maintain the Veil, of the vigilance required to ward off the encroaching chaos, and of the immense personal cost.

"We are nearing the site," Kael's voice resonated, tinged with a solemnity that echoed the somber beauty of their surroundings. "The Citadel of Whispers. It was once a nexus of immense power, a place where the Elder Weavers and their most gifted disciples worked to fortify the Veil. Your parents spent significant time here, Elara, honing their understanding of its delicate weave, preparing for the very threat we now face."

The mist thickened as they approached their destination, coalescing into spectral shapes that danced at the edges of Elara's vision. They were not solid entities, but rather ephemeral manifestations of energy, like heat haze made visible. Kael explained that these were residual echoes of powerful spells, lingering impressions of the beings who had once walked these hallowed grounds. Some were benign, remnants of protective enchantments, while others carried a faint, unsettling malevolence, echoes of desperate defenses against incursions from the shadowed realms.

The ground beneath Elara's feet began to change, the soft loam giving way to smooth, grey stone that was cracked and weathered by eons of exposure. The mist parted, not entirely, but enough to reveal the skeletal remains of immense structures. Towers, once proud and piercing the heavens, now sagged like broken teeth. Archways, intricately carved with celestial patterns, stood incomplete, their stones eroded into abstract, mournful shapes. This was the Citadel of Whispers, a monument to a forgotten age, a testament to a battle fought on a cosmic scale.

As Elara stepped through a gaping maw that had once been a grand entrance, a palpable wave of energy washed over her. It was not an aggressive force, but rather a resonant hum, a vibration that seemed to emanate from the very stones of the citadel. It felt ancient, potent, and deeply familiar. The locket around her neck grew warmer, its intricate carvings pulsing with a soft, internal luminescence. It was reacting to the ambient magic, to the residual power of her ancestors.

"The Citadel was built upon a convergence point of ley lines," Kael explained, his mental voice a steady beacon in the swirling energies. "These lines of natural magical power were harnessed and amplified by the Elder Weavers, allowing them to perform feats of creation and preservation on a scale unimaginable to most. Here, the Veil was not merely maintained; it was actively woven, its threads strengthened and its integrity reinforced."

Elara's gaze swept across the ruins. Crumbling courtyards lay choked with spectral flora, their luminescence casting an eerie glow on the decaying architecture. In the center of a vast, circular plaza, a shattered crystalline structure lay in pieces, its fragments still emitting faint, rainbow-colored sparks. Kael indicated that this had once been a focusing lens, used to channel and direct the energies of the ley lines, a tool of immense power now lying broken.

As Elara moved deeper into the citadel, the whispers intensified, no longer fleeting impressions but more coherent, albeit fragmented, streams of thought. They were the thoughts of the citadel's former guardians, their anxieties, their triumphs, their despair. She saw flashes of her parents, not as they were in the locket's fragmented visions, but as figures of immense power and focus, their hands tracing incandescent patterns in the air, their voices chanting words of binding and protection. The very air thrummed with their spectral presence.

"Your parents were deeply connected to this place." Kael's voice was soft, almost reverent. "They understood that the Veil was not a static barrier, but a living entity, constantly in need of care and reinforcement. They learned from the echoes left behind by the Elder Weavers, their knowledge etched into the very fabric of this citadel. The locket you wear... it is not merely a repository of their memories, but a key, attuned to the energies of this place. It amplifies your connection, allowing you to perceive what others cannot."

Elara reached out and touched a moss-covered obelisk. As her fingers made contact, a surge of images flooded her mind. She saw the Elder Weavers, beings of pure light and intricate form, their movements like a dance, their hands weaving threads of cosmic energy. She saw them crafting the Veil, not with hammer and chisel, but with song and intention, their collective will shaping the boundaries between worlds. Then, the images shifted, showing her parents working alongside these spectral figures, their own human forms imbued with an otherworldly glow, participating in the ancient ritual of mending.

The locket pulsed again, and this time, a distinct sensation flowed from it into Elara's mind. It was a feeling of profound understanding, a sudden, intuitive grasp of the principles of Veil weaving. She understood, in a way that transcended mere intellectual knowledge, the complex interplay of energies, the delicate balance that held reality together. It was as if a thousand years of accumulated wisdom had been condensed and poured directly into her consciousness.

"The Citadel itself acts as a conduit," Kael explained. "It amplifies the residual energies of those who were deeply connected to it. Your parents, in their dedication and their sacrifice, left an indelible mark. Their essence, their knowledge, is woven into the very stones of this place. By being here, by attuning yourself to the locket, you are awakening those echoes, drawing upon their legacy."

Elara found herself drawn to a central chamber, its ceiling a shattered dome that offered a glimpse of the perpetually overcast sky. In the center of the room, a raised platform held a single, ornate pedestal. It was empty, but Elara felt an overwhelming sense of purpose emanating from it, as if it were waiting for something – or someone. The whispers here were more insistent, coalescing into a chorus of encouragement and expectation.

"This was the heart of the Citadel's weaving chamber," Kael revealed. "The focal point from which the most intricate mending rituals were performed. Your parents often worked from this very spot. The locket... it resonates with a specific purpose here. It contains the fragmented blueprints of a particular sealing ritual, one designed to reinforce the Veil at its weakest points. But it requires a catalyst, a living conduit to channel the ambient energies and the latent power of your lineage."

Elara looked at the locket, then at the pedestal. The pieces were beginning to fall into place. Her journey here, the intensifying whispers, the surge of inherited knowledge – it was all leading to this moment. She understood now that her parents had not simply died to contain a threat; they had left behind the means to actively combat it. The Citadel of Whispers was not just a ruin; it was a training ground, a sanctuary of ancestral power.

She stepped onto the pedestal, the stone cool beneath her feet. As she stood there, the locket felt like a living thing against her chest, its warmth spreading through her. She closed her eyes, focusing on the whispers, on the images of her parents, on the newfound understanding of the Veil. She visualized the intricate weave, the shimmering threads of light and order, and the encroaching tendrils of darkness.

"Focus, Elara," Kael urged gently. "Feel the citadel's power, feel your parents' presence. The locket will guide you. It will show you the patterns, the intentions. You must replicate them, not with your hands, but with your will, with your very essence."

A soft light began to emanate from the locket, bathing Elara in its gentle glow. The whispers coalesced into a melody, a complex, ancient song of creation and preservation. Elara began to hum along, her voice trembling at first, then growing stronger, harmonizing with the spectral chorus. As she hummed, she visualized the patterns Kael had shown her, the intricate geometries of the Veil. She felt the ley lines beneath the citadel, pulsing with raw, untamed energy.

She raised her hands, not in a gesture of defiance, but of invitation. She willed the ambient energy to flow through her, through the locket, and into the waiting void above the pedestal. It was a terrifying act, surrendering herself to the torrent of power, but the legacy of her parents, the imperative to protect her world, fueled her resolve.

The air crackled with energy. The spectral flora around them pulsed brighter, and the broken crystalline fragments of the focusing lens flared with renewed intensity. Elara felt a connection forming, not just to the citadel, but to the Veil itself. It was a sensation of immense pressure, of countless points of vulnerability, but also of an inherent resilience, a desperate will to endure.

She saw in her mind's eye the intricate dance of weaving, the precise movements required to mend a tear, to reinforce a weakened thread. Her parents' spectral forms flickered into existence around her, their faces etched with concentration, their hands moving in perfect synchronicity with hers, though they were not physically present. They were guiding her, sharing their muscle memory, their spiritual intent.

The ritual was not one of aggression, but of profound, focused repair. Elara was not attacking the encroaching darkness, but rather strengthening the existing structure, making it more resilient. She was weaving, not with physical thread, but with pure intent, with the focused energy of her lineage, amplified by the Citadel and the locket.

She felt the locket surge with power, a miniature sun against her chest. The energy flowing through her was immense, almost overwhelming, but she held on, anchoring herself to the echoes of her parents' love and their unwavering dedication. The whispers within the citadel shifted, transforming from a chorus of expectation to a song of fulfillment, of connection. They were the echoes of the Veil itself, recognizing her touch, her intent.

The process felt timeless, yet it was over in an instant. As the surge of energy subsided, Elara felt drained, but also invigorated. The locket's glow softened, its warmth now a comforting reassurance. The spectral figures of her parents faded, leaving behind a sense of profound peace.

"You have done well, Elara," Kael's voice was filled with a quiet pride. "You have embraced the legacy. The Citadel of Whispers has shared its secrets, and you have proven yourself a worthy inheritor of your parents' power and purpose. The mending has begun."

Elara looked at her hands, expecting to see them glowing, but they were unchanged. Yet, she felt different. A deeper understanding of the world, of its fragility and its interconnectedness, had settled within her. The echoes of her parents were no longer just fragments in a locket; they were now a living part of her. The Citadel had not just shown her the path; it had imbued her with the ability to walk it. She had felt the Veil, touched its intricate weave, and in doing so, had begun the arduous but vital task of its preservation. The ruins around her, once symbols of decay, now felt like a testament to enduring strength, a place where the past continued to shape the future. The whispers, once filled with foreboding, now carried a note of hope, a quiet assurance that even in the face of overwhelming darkness, the threads of light could be woven anew.

The residual magic of the Citadel, once a comforting hum resonating with her lineage, now began to fray at the edges. Elara, still basking in the afterglow of her ritual, felt a prickling unease, a subtle shift in the charged atmosphere. It was as if the very air had grown heavy, tainted with a chill that had nothing to do with the mist or the age of the ruins. Kael's voice, usually a steady presence, carried a note of sharp vigilance. "Elara, the Shadow Lord senses your awakening. Your communion with the Veil has not gone unnoticed."

As if on cue, the ethereal glow that had suffused the chamber began to dim, not fading, but being choked by creeping shadows. They were not the familiar twilight gloom of the Citadel, but something more profound, more invasive. Tendrils of inky blackness began to snake across the stone floor, coiling around the spectral flora, snuffing out their soft luminescence. They moved with a liquid grace, each ripple of their passage accompanied by a faint, insidious whisper that seemed to claw at the edges of Elara's mind. These were not the echoes of the Citadel's guardians, nor the sorrowful laments of the Veil. These were venomous suggestions, fragments of doubt designed to fester.

"Weak," a voice, slithering and cold, whispered directly into her thoughts. *"You are a pale imitation. Your parents failed. You will fail, too."*

Elara flinched, her hand instinctively going to the locket. The warmth was still there, a solid anchor, but the tendrils of darkness seemed to writhe with a perverse delight at her reaction. She could feel them probing, seeking any crack in her resolve, any vulnerability to exploit. The images of her parents, so clear and comforting moments before, began to warp in her memory, their faces contorted into expressions of fear, their spectral forms dissolving into ash.

"Do not listen, Elara," Kael's voice was firm, a lifeline in the encroaching murk. "These are illusions, projections of your deepest fears. The Shadow Lord feeds on despair. You must not give him a purchase."

But it was easier said than done. The whispers grew more insistent, weaving themselves into the fabric of her very being. They spoke of her isolation, of the weight of responsibility that rested solely on her young shoulders. They painted vivid pictures of the world outside, of its impending doom, of the futility of her efforts. Each word was a tiny barb, designed to pierce her spirit.

"They all abandoned you," another voice, this one laced with a mocking sympathy, insinuated. *"Kael, your parents… they all knew you were insufficient. They left you to face this alone. This Citadel, this power… It's a mockery. You are nothing."*

Elara stumbled back, her breath catching in her throat. The shadows intensified, their tendrils reaching out, not to touch her physically, but to wrap around her thoughts, her emotions. She felt a wave of profound loneliness wash over her, a crushing sense of insignificance. The vibrant legacy she had just embraced felt hollow, a cruel trick. She saw herself as a child, forgotten and overlooked, and the specter of that vulnerability loomed large.

"No," she whispered, the word barely audible. "That's not true."

"Isn't it?" the voices slithered back, more confident now. *"Look at you. Trembling. Alone. What can you possibly do? You are just a girl playing with powers you don't understand. The Veil is fraying. The Shadow Lord is coming. And you... You are not strong enough to stop him."*

The darkness pulsed, and in its depths, Elara saw a fleeting, terrifying vision: the world she knew consumed by an all-encompassing blackness, her loved ones dissolving into nothingness, her own screams unheard. The sheer despair of the vision threatened to suffocate her. She felt the icy grip of hopelessness begin to tighten, the insidious promise of oblivion whispering a siren song of release.

Kael's presence, though not physically manifest, felt like a steady hand on her shoulder. "Remember your training, Elara. Remember the principles of the Veil. It is not a static shield, but a living weave. And you, child of the Elder Weavers, are a weaver. Your power is not in brute force, but in resilience, in mending, in the strength of your intention."

Elara closed her eyes, forcing herself to block out the insidious whispers. She recalled the moments of clarity she had experienced on the pedestal, the intuitive understanding of the Veil's intricate patterns. She remembered the spectral forms of her parents, their unwavering focus, their quiet determination. They had faced this darkness, and they had not yielded. Their legacy was not just power, but courage.

She focused on the locket, feeling its steady warmth against her skin. It was more than just a repository of memories; it was a conduit, a symbol of her connection to those who had come before. She imagined the threads of the Veil, not as fragile strands, but as incredibly strong, interwoven cords of light and energy, constantly being reinforced. The Shadow Lord's tendrils were attempts to sever those cords, to unravel the tapestry of existence. But what if she could use his own darkness against him? What if she could weave his disruptive energy into the fabric of the Veil, not to strengthen it, but to reinforce its very structure, to make it more resilient to his attacks?

"Foolish," the whispers sneered, sensing her shift in focus. *"You cannot control what you do not understand. His power will consume you."*

"I am not trying to control it," Elara thought back, her inner voice gaining strength. "I am integrating it. The Veil is a reflection of all energies, even the darkness. To deny it is to weaken it. To understand it, to weave it into the existing tapestry... that is true strength."

She began to visualize the tendrils of darkness not as enemies, but as raw, chaotic energy. They were untamed, disruptive, but not inherently destructive. Their destruction came from their unchecked proliferation, their ability to sow discord. She pictured them as dark threads, rough and tangled, but threads nonetheless. She imagined pulling them towards the center of the weaving chamber, towards the nexus of power where she had stood moments before.

With a deep breath, Elara opened her mind to the encroaching shadows. She felt their cold, alien nature, their utter lack of empathy. But she also felt their immense, raw power. Instead of recoiling, she embraced it, drawing it into herself, not to be corrupted, but to be understood. It was an agonizing process, like swallowing shards of ice, each one searing her soul. But she held on, anchoring herself to the image of her parents, to the echoes of their sacrifice.

Kael's voice, though still distant, sounded impressed. "Remarkable, Elara. You are not fighting the darkness; you are embracing its nature. You are weaving with it, not against it."

As she drew the shadowy tendrils closer, Elara began to hum. It was not the ancient song of the Citadel, but a new melody, one born of her own resilience and her willingness to face the void. Her hum was low, a counterpoint to the insidious whispers, a steady vibration that seemed to resonate with the very structure of reality. She visualized the dark threads weaving themselves into the intricate patterns of the Veil, not as tears or weaknesses, but as integral components, adding depth and complexity.

The spectral tendrils, instead of overwhelming her, began to respond to her will. They coiled around her, not constricting, but weaving, guided by her intention. It felt as if she were pulling on invisible threads, drawing them into a cosmic loom. The Citadel seemed to respond to her efforts, the residual magic flaring anew, not in opposition to the encroaching darkness, but in harmony with it. The broken crystalline fragments on the floor pulsed with a renewed, darker light, reflecting the twisted energies she was now manipulating.

The whispers of doubt and despair began to falter, replaced by a confused dissonance. They were losing their hold, their power diminished by Elara's deliberate integration of the Shadow Lord's influence.

"This is not possible," the primary voice of the Shadow Lord, now more palpable and enraged, boomed in her mind. It was a sound of grinding stone and screaming void. *"You cannot comprehend my power! You are merely a vessel, a temporary conduit for a force you cannot truly grasp!"*

"Perhaps," Elara thought, her inner voice now calm and resolute. "But I can weave. And this weave is becoming stronger, more resilient, precisely because it acknowledges the darkness. You sought to break me with fear, but you have only taught me how to mend with it."

She felt a surge of power unlike anything before. It was not the pure, radiant energy of the Citadel, but a potent, volatile force, tempered by her own will. She was not merely reinforcing the Veil; she was making it more complex, more capable of withstanding the Shadow Lord's attacks by incorporating his own essence into its structure. It was a dangerous gambit, like holding a volatile alchemical mixture, but her lineage, her training, and her sheer determination allowed her to maintain control.

She visualized the Veil as a vast, shimmering tapestry, and the Shadow Lord's tendrils as dark, twisted threads. Instead of trying to burn them away, she was carefully weaving them into the existing patterns, creating new designs, new strengths. Where once there were tears and weaknesses, there were now intricate, dark knots, adding resilience and a deeper complexity to the Veil. It was a profound act of transformation, turning the Shadow Lord's own weapon against him.

The process was physically and mentally draining. Elara felt as though her very essence was being stretched thin, pulled in a thousand directions. Sweat beaded on her forehead, and her muscles trembled with exertion. But she saw the effect of her actions. The encroaching shadows around her began to recede, not vanishing entirely, but becoming less menacing, less invasive. They were no longer a direct assault, but a subtle, integrated element within the Citadel's ambient magic.

Kael's voice was laced with awe. "You have done it, Elara. You have faced the Shadow Lord's influence and turned it into a source of strength. You have woven the very essence of his corruption into the Veil, making it more resilient than ever before. This… this is a power beyond anything I had imagined."

Elara finally allowed herself to release the intense focus. The dark tendrils ceased their active weaving and settled into the ambient magic, no longer an immediate threat, but a subtle undercurrent. The Citadel's light returned, brighter than before, as if invigorated by the integration of these new energies. The whispers of doubt and despair were gone, replaced by a steady, resonant hum of power and resilience.

She sank to her knees, the locket still warm against her chest. The battle had been internal, a fierce struggle waged within the confines of her own mind and spirit. But its impact was tangible, a new layer of strength woven into the very fabric of reality. She had confronted the Shadow Lord's insidious grasp and emerged not unscathed, but stronger, her understanding of the Veil deepened, her resolve solidified. She had not merely defended; she had evolved, transforming a threat into a testament to her own growing power and the enduring strength of the legacy she carried. The shadows had not consumed her; they had become a part of her, a reminder that even in the deepest darkness, there could be found the seeds of resilience and the potential for profound transformation. The Citadel had not just revealed its secrets; it had tested her, and in doing so, had forged her into something new, something more.

The air in the chamber, which had thrummed with a potent, yet reassuring magic moments before, now seemed to hold a new tension. The residual power of the Citadel, once a comforting hum resonating with Elara's lineage, had begun to fray at the edges, an unsettling shift that prickled her unease. Kael's voice, typically a steady anchor, now carried a sharp note of vigilance. "Elara," he had warned, his voice a low rumble against the fading echoes of her connection to the Veil, "the Shadow Lord senses your awakening. Your communion with the Veil has not gone unnoticed."

As if responding to his words, the ethereal glow that had suffused the chamber began to dim, not fading, but being choked by creeping shadows. These were not the familiar twilight gloom of the ancient ruins, but something more profound, more invasive. Tendrils of inky blackness snaked across the stone floor, coiling around the spectral flora, snuffing out their soft luminescence. They moved with a liquid grace, each ripple of their passage accompanied by a faint, insidious whisper that clawed at the edges of Elara's mind. These were not the echoes of the Citadel's guardians, nor the sorrowful laments of the Veil. These were venomous suggestions, fragments of doubt designed to fester.

"Weak," a voice, slithering and cold, whispered directly into her thoughts. *"You are a pale imitation. Your parents failed. You will fail, too."*

Elara flinched, her hand instinctively going to the locket. Its warmth was still there, a solid anchor, but the tendrils of darkness seemed to writhe with a perverse delight at her reaction. She felt them probing, seeking any crack in her resolve, any vulnerability to exploit. The images of her parents, so clear and comforting moments before, began to warp in her memory, their faces contorted into expressions of fear, their spectral forms dissolving into ash.

"Do not listen, Elara," Kael's voice was firm, a lifeline in the encroaching murk. "These are illusions, projections of your deepest fears. The Shadow Lord feeds on despair. You must not give him a purchase."

But it was easier said than done. The whispers grew more insistent, weaving themselves into the fabric of her very being. They spoke of her isolation, of the weight of responsibility that rested solely on her young shoulders. They painted vivid pictures of the world outside, of its impending doom, of the futility of her efforts. Each word was a tiny barb, designed to pierce her spirit.

163

"They all abandoned you," another voice, this one laced with a mocking sympathy, insinuated. *"Kael, your parents... they all knew you were insufficient. They left you to face this alone. This Citadel, this power... It's a mockery. You are nothing."*

Elara stumbled back, her breath catching in her throat. The shadows intensified, their tendrils reaching out, not to touch her physically, but to wrap around her thoughts, her emotions. She felt a wave of profound loneliness wash over her, a crushing sense of insignificance. The vibrant legacy she had just embraced felt hollow, a cruel trick. She saw herself as a child, forgotten and overlooked, and the specter of that vulnerability loomed large.

"No," she whispered, the word barely audible. "That's not true."

"Isn't it?" the voices slithered back, more confident now. *"Look at you. Trembling. Alone. What can you possibly do? You are just a girl playing with powers you don't understand. The Veil is fraying. The Shadow Lord is coming. And you... You are not strong enough to stop him."*

The darkness pulsed, and in its depths, Elara saw a fleeting, terrifying vision: the world she knew consumed by an all-encompassing blackness, her loved ones dissolving into nothingness, her own screams unheard. The sheer despair of the vision threatened to suffocate her. She felt the icy grip of hopelessness begin to tighten, the insidious promise of oblivion whispering a siren song of release.

Kael's presence, though not physically manifest, felt like a steady hand on her shoulder. "Remember your training, Elara. Remember the principles of the Veil. It is not a static shield, but a living weave. And you, child of the Elder Weavers, are a weaver. Your power is not in brute force, but in resilience, in mending, in the strength of your intention."

Elara closed her eyes, forcing herself to block out the insidious whispers. She recalled the moments of clarity she had experienced on the pedestal, the intuitive understanding of the Veil's intricate patterns. She remembered the spectral forms of her parents, their unwavering focus, their quiet determination. They had faced this darkness, and they had not yielded. Their legacy was not just power, but courage.

She focused on the locket, feeling its steady warmth against her skin. It was more than just a repository of memories; it was a conduit, a symbol of her connection to those who had come before. She imagined the threads of the Veil, not as fragile strands, but as incredibly strong, interwoven cords of light and energy, constantly being reinforced. The Shadow Lord's tendrils were attempts to sever those cords, to unravel the tapestry of existence. But what if she could use his own darkness against him? What if she could weave his disruptive energy into the fabric of the Veil, not to strengthen it, but to reinforce its very structure, to make it more resilient to his attacks?

"Foolish," the whispers sneered, sensing her shift in focus. *"You cannot control what you do not understand. His power will consume you."*

"I am not trying to control it," Elara thought back, her inner voice gaining strength. "I am integrating it. The Veil is a reflection of all energies, even the darkness. To deny it is to weaken it. To understand it, to weave it into the existing tapestry... that is true strength."

She began to visualize the tendrils of darkness not as enemies, but as raw, chaotic energy. They were untamed, disruptive, but not inherently destructive. Their destruction came from their unchecked proliferation, their ability to sow discord. She pictured them as dark threads, rough and tangled, but threads nonetheless. She imagined pulling them towards the center of the weaving chamber, towards the nexus of power where she had stood moments before.

With a deep breath, Elara opened her mind to the encroaching shadows. She felt their cold, alien nature, their utter lack of empathy. But she also felt their immense, raw power. Instead of recoiling, she embraced it, drawing it into herself, not to be corrupted, but to be understood. It was an agonizing process, like swallowing shards of ice, each one searing her soul. But she held on, anchoring herself to the image of her parents, to the echoes of their sacrifice.

Kael's voice, though still distant, sounded impressed. "Remarkable, Elara. You are not fighting the darkness; you are embracing its nature. You are weaving with it, not against it."

As she drew the shadowy tendrils closer, Elara began to hum. It was not the ancient song of the Citadel, but a new melody, one born of her own resilience and her willingness to face the void. Her hum was low, a counterpoint to the insidious whispers, a steady vibration that seemed to resonate with the very structure of reality. She visualized the dark threads weaving themselves into the intricate patterns of the Veil, not as tears or weaknesses, but as integral components, adding depth and complexity.

The spectral tendrils, instead of overwhelming her, began to respond to her will. They coiled around her, not constricting, but weaving, guided by her intention. It felt as if she were pulling on invisible threads, drawing them into a cosmic loom. The Citadel seemed to respond to her efforts, the residual magic flaring anew, not in opposition to the encroaching darkness, but in harmony with it. The broken crystalline fragments on the floor pulsed with a renewed, darker light, reflecting the twisted energies she was now manipulating.

The whispers of doubt and despair began to falter, replaced by a confused dissonance. They were losing their hold, their power diminished by Elara's deliberate integration of the Shadow Lord's influence.

166

"This is not possible," the primary voice of the Shadow Lord, now more palpable and enraged, boomed in her mind. It was a sound of grinding stone and screaming void. *"You cannot comprehend my power! You are merely a vessel, a temporary conduit for a force you cannot truly grasp!"*

"Perhaps," Elara thought, her inner voice now calm and resolute. "But I can weave. And this weave is becoming stronger, more resilient, precisely because it acknowledges the darkness. You sought to break me with fear, but you have only taught me how to mend with it."

She felt a surge of power unlike anything before. It was not the pure, radiant energy of the Citadel, but a potent, volatile force, tempered by her own will. She was not merely reinforcing the Veil; she was making it more complex, more capable of withstanding the Shadow Lord's attacks by incorporating his own essence into its structure. It was a dangerous gambit, like holding a volatile alchemical mixture, but her lineage, her training, and her sheer determination allowed her to maintain control.

She visualized the Veil as a vast, shimmering tapestry, and the Shadow Lord's tendrils as dark, twisted threads. Instead of trying to burn them away, she was carefully weaving them into the existing patterns, creating new designs, new strengths. Where once there were tears and weaknesses, there were now intricate, dark knots, adding resilience and a deeper complexity to the Veil. It was a profound act of transformation, turning the Shadow Lord's own weapon against him.

The process was physically and mentally draining. Elara felt as though her very essence was being stretched thin, pulled in a thousand directions. Sweat beaded on her forehead, and her muscles trembled with exertion. But she saw the effect of her actions. The encroaching shadows around her began to recede, not vanishing entirely, but becoming less menacing, less invasive. They were no longer a direct assault, but a subtle, integrated element within the Citadel's ambient magic.

Kael's voice was laced with awe. "You have done it, Elara. You have faced the Shadow Lord's influence and turned it into a source of strength. You have woven the very essence of his corruption into the Veil, making it more resilient than ever before. This... this is a power beyond anything I had imagined."

Elara finally allowed herself to release the intense focus. The dark tendrils ceased their active weaving and settled into the ambient magic, no longer an immediate threat, but a subtle undercurrent. The Citadel's light returned, brighter than before, as if invigorated by the integration of these new energies. The whispers of doubt and despair were gone, replaced by a steady, resonant hum of power and resilience.

She sank to her knees, the locket still warm against her chest. The battle had been internal, a fierce struggle waged within the confines of her own mind and spirit. But its impact was tangible, a new layer of strength woven into the very fabric of reality. She had confronted the Shadow Lord's insidious grasp and emerged not unscathed, but stronger, her understanding of the Veil deepened, her resolve solidified. She had not merely defended; she had evolved, transforming a threat into a testament to her own growing power and the enduring strength of the legacy she carried. The shadows had not consumed her; they had become a part of her, a reminder that even in the deepest darkness, there could be found the seeds of resilience and the potential for profound transformation. The Citadel had not just revealed its secrets; it had tested her, and in doing so, had forged her into something new, something more.

Kael's voice, now imbued with a profound reverence, echoed through the revitalized chamber. "Elara, that was merely a prelude. What you have done today, while extraordinary, was an instinctive reaction to immediate danger. The ritual, the true ritual of sealing, is far more complex. It is a rite that has been passed down through your bloodline for generations, a sacred duty entrusted to the Elder Weavers. That locket you wear is not merely a memento of your parents, nor just a key. It is the central focus, the very heart of this ancient ceremony."

He explained that the Veil, the ethereal barrier between worlds that protected their realm from the encroaching darkness, was not a static construct. It was a living tapestry, constantly under siege from the malevolent forces of the Shadow Lord. While individual acts of magic, like the one she had just performed, could reinforce its structure, the annual ritual was crucial for its long-term integrity. It was a proactive defense, a deliberate act of strengthening the Veil against the inevitable tides of corruption.

"Your parents," Kael continued, his voice softening with a hint of sorrow and immense pride, "they performed this ritual every year. It was a sacred duty, one that demanded their complete focus, their deepest reserves of power, and their unwavering connection to the Veil. They would use the locket, channeling their magic through it, to weave in protective energies, to mend the unseen tears caused by the Shadow Lord's influence, and to push back the creeping tendrils of his power. It was their legacy, Elara, a legacy now passed to you."

Elara listened, her mind reeling, yet a sense of understanding began to dawn. The raw, chaotic magic she had felt surging within her, the volatile energies she had managed to tame, were precisely the kind of forces needed for such a ritual. The Shadow Lord's attempts to corrupt and destroy were, in essence, the raw materials. Her ability to integrate that darkness, to weave it into the existing fabric, was the key to performing the sealing rite.

"But the ritual itself," Kael elaborated, "is not simply about channeling power. It is about intention, about understanding the intricate dance of creation and destruction, light and shadow. It requires a deep communion with the Veil, not just as a magical construct, but as a living entity. You must become one with its currents, feel it's every pulse, and guide its energies with absolute clarity of purpose. The locket acts as an amplifier, a conduit that allows you to channel not only your own magic but also the ancestral magic of your lineage, the very essence of the Elder Weavers who first established this rite."

He described the locket as a vessel of woven starlight and solidified intent, imbued with the echoes of countless generations of Weavers who had performed the sealing. It resonated with the very soul of the Veil, amplifying Elara's will and focusing her magic into a precise, directed force. Without it, any attempt to perform the full ritual would be like trying to redirect a river with bare hands – a futile and potentially dangerous endeavor.

"The ritual requires you to stand at the heart of this Citadel, at the nexus of power," Kael explained, his voice taking on a measured, instructional tone. "You must place the locket upon the central altar, which you may have noticed during your earlier communion. Then, you will draw upon the energies that surround you, the residual magic of this place, the very essence of the Veil itself. But most importantly, you will draw upon the power within you, the power that has awakened in your blood. The chaotic magic you have recently experienced? That is the raw essence of the Shadow Lord's influence, the very thing you must contend with. Your task is to channel this volatile energy, not to destroy it, but to refine it, to weave it into the Veil in a way that strengthens its structure, making it more resistant to his future incursions."

Elara's mind raced, trying to grasp the immense implications of Kael's words. This wasn't just about defending; it was about actively engaging with the enemy's power, transforming his chaos into a bulwark. It was a dangerous undertaking, a tightrope walk over an abyss. The whispers of doubt and fear, which had seemed to recede, now resurfaced in her mind, albeit fainter. *What if I fail? What if I can't control it? What if I become corrupted?*

Kael seemed to sense her apprehension. "The path of the Elder Weaver is never easy, Elara. It demands courage, resilience, and an unwavering commitment to the balance. You have already shown an extraordinary capacity to face the darkness, to understand it, and to integrate it. That is the first, and perhaps most crucial, step. The locket will guide you. Your parents' spirit will be with you. And I will be here, offering what guidance I can. But the ultimate strength, the decision to embrace this legacy and perform the ritual, must come from you."

He then began to detail the steps of the ritual, his words painting a vivid picture in Elara's mind. The ritual was not a single act, but a sequence of intricate magical weaving, each step building upon the last. It involved tracing specific sigils on the altar with the locket, each sigil representing a different aspect of the Veil's integrity: resilience, clarity, protection, and balance. As she traced these sigils, she would need to visualize the corresponding energies flowing from the locket, infusing the very stones of the Citadel and extending outwards to mend the Veil.

"The most critical phase," Kael emphasized, "is the channeling of the Shadow Lord's influence. You will feel it, Elara. You will feel it's cold, hungry pull. It will try to consume you, to twist your intent. You must resist that urge. Do not fight it with raw power; fight it with understanding. See it not as an enemy to be vanquished, but as a chaotic force to be integrated, like a dark thread woven into a luminous tapestry. You must use the locket to guide that thread, to ensure it reinforces, rather than tears, the fabric of the Veil. It is a delicate balance, a dance between opposing forces. Your intention must be pure: to protect, to mend, to preserve the balance."

He spoke of the incantations, ancient words of power that resonated with the very foundations of their world, words that had been whispered by Elder Weavers for millennia. These were not mere words, but keys that unlocked deeper levels of magical potential, words that shaped reality itself. Elara would need to recite them with conviction, with the full force of her will behind each syllable.

"The echoes of your parents' efforts will be present," Kael assured her, "not as a burden, but as a source of strength. You will feel their connection to the locket, their guiding presence. Remember their bravery, Elara. Remember their sacrifice. They faced this threat time and again, and they did not falter. You carry their blood, their lineage, and their duty. This ritual is your inheritance, your responsibility, and your greatest trial."

He explained that the success of the ritual was not guaranteed. It depended on her focus, her courage, and her ability to master the volatile energies that now coursed through her. A single misstep, a moment of doubt, could have catastrophic consequences, potentially weakening the Veil further or, worse, allowing the Shadow Lord's influence to seep through.

"The ritual must be performed during the convergence," Kael stated, his gaze intense. "The next convergence is imminent, within days. You must be prepared. The Citadel will serve as your sanctuary, your training ground. We will practice, Elara. We will work through the steps, refine your control, and strengthen your resolve. You must embrace this legacy, not as a burden, but as your destiny. The fate of the Veil, and perhaps the world, rests on your willingness to perform the Ritual of Sealing."

Elara stood, the weight of his words settling upon her. The residual magic of the Citadel, which had seemed so chaotic moments before, now felt like a tangible power waiting to be shaped. The locket around her neck felt heavier, a symbol of both her heritage and her future. The fear was still present, a cold knot in her stomach, but it was now tempered by a growing sense of purpose. She looked at the altar, the place where she had felt the first stirrings of her lineage's power. It was here, she knew, that she would need to stand, to face the darkness, and to embrace the daunting, vital duty of the Elder Weaver. Her parents had passed on their legacy not just in power, but in responsibility, and it was time for her to truly inherit it. The ritual was not an option; it was the culmination of everything that had brought her to this place, to this moment. She was the inheritor, and the Veil awaited her touch.

The chamber hummed with an energy that was both ancient and vibrantly new, a symphony of power that resonated deep within Elara's bones. The locket, a constant warmth against her skin, pulsed in time with the Citadel's own magical heart. Kael's words, echoing in the newly quieted space, painted a stark picture of her inheritance: the Ritual of Sealing, a sacred duty passed down through generations of Elder Weavers. It was not merely an act of magic, but a testament to sacrifice, a continuous battle waged against the encroaching darkness of the Shadow Lord. Elara understood, with a clarity that settled like a heavy cloak upon her shoulders, that her parents had not simply died; they had given their lives, year after year, to maintain the Veil, the very fabric separating their world from oblivion.

As Kael began to guide her through the initial stages of the ritual, the altar at the chamber's center pulsed with a soft, pearlescent light. It was more than just a stone slab; it was a nexus, a focal point designed to amplify and direct the immense energies involved. Elara placed the locket upon it, its familiar weight now imbued with the gravity of her impending task. The metal felt cool beneath her fingers, yet a tremor of latent power ran through it, a testament to the countless times it had been held by her ancestors. She could almost feel their presence, a spectral chorus whispering encouragement and caution.

"Each sigil you trace," Kael's voice was a steady murmur, "represents a fundamental aspect of the Veil's strength. Resilience. Clarity. Protection. Balance. Focus your intent, Elara. Visualize these energies flowing not just from the locket, but from the very essence of your being, seeping into the Citadel's foundations and radiating outwards."

With a deep breath, Elara traced the first sigil, a complex knot of interwoven lines that seemed to mirror the intricate patterns of the

173

Veil itself. As her finger, guided by the locket, moved across the stone, a soft luminescence bloomed beneath her touch. It spread, a gentle tide of golden light, filling the chamber with a palpable sense of peace. She felt a connection forming, not just to the Citadel, but to the world beyond its walls, a world that slept, unaware of the precarious shield that protected it. The whispers of her parents, once spectral and distant, grew clearer, their voices now carrying a deeper resonance, imbued with the memories of this very place, this very ritual.

The second sigil, one of sharp angles and radiating lines, evoked a sense of unwavering resolve. As she traced it, the golden light intensified, shifting to a brilliant sapphire, sharp and piercing. Elara felt a surge of defensive energy, a primal instinct to shield and protect. The whispers of the Shadow Lord, which had momentarily retreated, flickered at the edges of her awareness, a faint, chilling breeze against the warmth of the Citadel's magic. They were a reminder of the constant threat, the unseen enemy that perpetually gnawed at the Veil.

"You are doing well, Elara," Kael said, his voice a blend of admiration and urgency. "But now comes the true test. You must draw upon the Shadow Lord's influence, not to wield it, but to integrate it. This is where your unique understanding becomes paramount."

As Kael spoke of the Shadow Lord's influence, the very air in the chamber seemed to thicken, growing heavy and oppressive. The sapphire light flickered, momentarily giving way to tendrils of an inky, corrosive darkness. Elara felt its presence immediately, a cold, alien hunger that sought to latch onto her, to twist her intent. It was a force of pure entropy, the antithesis of the Veil's protective weaving.

"Do not resist it with brute force," Kael urged. "See it as raw material, as a dark thread. Your task is to weave it, to incorporate it into the tapestry of the Veil, reinforcing its structure, not tearing it asunder."

Elara focused on the locket, its surface now feeling strangely warm, almost volatile, as it reacted to the encroaching darkness. She closed her eyes, picturing the Veil not as a uniform shield, but as an infinitely complex weave, a tapestry of light and shadow, creation and dissolution. The Shadow Lord's power was the embodiment of that dissolution, and in a twisted sense, it was also a necessary component. For without the constant threat of unravelling, the act of weaving and reinforcing would lose its meaning.

She extended her hand, the locket leading the way, and reached out to the encroaching shadows. It was an act of profound courage, akin to walking into a blizzard with only a thin cloak. The darkness recoiled momentarily, as if surprised by her willingness to engage, but then surged forward, its tendrils lashing out, seeking to ensnare her. A wave of despair washed over her, a chilling reminder of her isolation, of the immense responsibility she now carried alone.

"You are not strong enough," the familiar insidious whispers slithered into her mind. *"This power is too great. You will be consumed."*

But Elara had faced these whispers before, in the heart of the Citadel. She remembered the strength she had found within herself, the resilience she had forged in the crucible of her own fears. She gripped the locket tighter, its ancient magic a bulwark against the encroaching despair.

"I am not fighting you," she projected mentally, her will a shield against the Shadow Lord's psychic assault. "I am integrating you. You are a part of the cosmic weave, just as light is. And I, Elara, daughter of the Elder Weavers, will ensure that your place in that weave serves to strengthen, not destroy."

As she spoke these words, a vision bloomed before her eyes, unbidden, yet impossibly real. It was not a vision of the Shadow Lord's desolate domain, nor of the world's imminent destruction. Instead, it was a scene of profound peace, a tranquil valley bathed in the soft, perpetual twilight of the Sundered Realm. Luminescent flora cast a gentle glow upon rolling hills, and crystalline streams meandered through meadows of iridescent grass. In the distance, nestled amongst the gentle slopes, stood a humble, elegant dwelling, its architecture reminiscent of the Citadel but softened, more inviting.

And there, Elara saw them. Her parents.

They were younger, their faces etched with a contentment she had only glimpsed in faded portraits. They walked hand-in-hand, their spectral forms now solid, vibrant, alive. They were not warriors, not guardians burdened by the weight of the world. They were simply... them. Laughing. Sharing a quiet moment beneath a sky filled with slow-moving, bioluminescent clouds. They seemed at peace, their spirits finally free from the relentless vigilance that had defined their lives. Elara felt a pang of longing so intense it threatened to steal her breath. This was what they had sacrificed. This idyllic existence, this quiet haven where they could finally be together, unbound by duty or danger.

The scene was so real, so tangible, that Elara could almost feel the soft breeze on her skin, smell the sweet, unfamiliar scent of the Sundered Realm's flora. A profound sadness washed over her, not for their loss, but for the life they had been denied, the life she herself might have lived had fate, or rather destiny, not intervened. The temptation to simply step into that vision, to embrace that peace, to join them in their quiet sanctuary, was overwhelming. It was a siren song of solace, a promise of an end to the struggle, an end to the fear.

"Come home, Elara," a gentle voice, her mother's, seemed to whisper from the vision. *"Join us. Your duty is done. Here, you can finally rest."*

The Shadow Lord's influence, which had been a torrent of chaotic energy, seemed to recede, replaced by this profound, seductive peace. The locket pulsed gently, almost as if urging her towards this vision of solace. It was a choice, stark and terrifying. She could embrace the Legacy, continue the arduous task of defending the Veil, a task that would undoubtedly demand more of her, perhaps even her life, just as it had claimed her parents'. Or she could step into this vision and find her own peace, abandoning the world to its fate.

Elara stood at a precipice, the raw power of the Shadow Lord a chaotic storm at her back, and the serene beauty of the Sundered Realm beckoning her forward. She saw herself walking towards her parents, their spectral forms reaching out to embrace her, their eyes filled with love and relief. The burdens she carried – the locket, the Citadel, the Veil, the fate of her world – all seemed to melt away with each step closer to that tranquil valley.

But as she neared the threshold of the vision, another voice, Kael's, cut through the comforting illusion. "Elara! Do not be swayed! This is a manifestation of your deepest desires, a temptation offered by the Shadow Lord to break your resolve!"

His words, though sharp, resonated with the truth she already knew. This vision of peace, of reunion, was a carefully crafted illusion. Her parents' sacrifice was not an invitation to join them in oblivion, but a testament to their unwavering commitment to protecting what they loved. They had fought to preserve the realm, to give others the chance to live in peace, not to escape it entirely. Their ultimate sacrifice was not an escape from their duty, but the culmination of it.

Elara's gaze shifted from the idyllic valley to the altar, the locket still warm in her hand. She saw the sigils she had traced, the sapphire light still radiating from them, a beacon of defiance. She felt the volatile energy of the Shadow Lord's influence, a force that could shatter worlds, but also a force that, when understood and woven, could strengthen the very fabric of existence.

Her parents had made their choice. They had chosen duty over personal solace. They had chosen the precarious protection of the Veil over the serene embrace of the Sundered Realm. And in doing so, they had given Elara the chance to live, the chance to grow, the chance to *become* the bridge between these worlds. To abandon that, to succumb to the temptation of personal peace, would be to negate their sacrifice, to render their struggle meaningless.

"No," Elara whispered, her voice gaining strength, her gaze hardening. She pulled her hand back from the alluring vision, the warmth of her parents' presence fading as she turned her focus back to the task at hand. The seductive peace of the Sundered Realm shimmered and began to dissipate, the illusions of the Shadow Lord dissolving under the force of her renewed resolve. "I cannot. Their sacrifice… it was to protect this world. To give others a chance at the peace they deserved. To abandon that would be a betrayal of everything they stood for."

The dark tendrils of the Shadow Lord's influence surged forward again, sensing her wavering. But this time, Elara met them not with fear, but with a profound understanding, a newfound acceptance of the burden. She saw the Shadow Lord's game: to offer solace, to tempt with escape, to break the will of those who stood as guardians. But her parents had taught her a greater lesson: true strength lay not in escape, but in acceptance, in embracing the responsibility, in weaving even the darkest threads into a tapestry of resilience.

She grasped the locket, its familiar weight now feeling like a conduit, not just to her parents' magic, but to their courage. The vision of the Sundered Realm faded entirely, replaced by the stark reality of the Citadel chamber, the altar, and the encroaching darkness. The echoes of her parents' love remained, not as a temptation to retreat, but as a wellspring of strength, a reminder of the legacy she was bound to uphold.

"You sought to break me with comfort," Elara projected mentally, her voice echoing with a new authority that resonated through the chamber. "But you only showed me what was worth fighting for. You showed me the immense love that fueled their sacrifice. And that love, that commitment to life, is a far greater force than any darkness you can conjure."

She began to trace the next sigil on the altar, a complex, spiraling pattern that spoke of the constant, dynamic flux of the Veil. As her fingers moved, guided by the locket, the dark tendrils of the Shadow Lord's influence did not recede. Instead, they seemed to writhe and twist, drawn to the locket's power, ready to be woven. Elara focused on the raw energy, the inherent chaos, and instead of recoiling, she embraced it, drawing it into herself, not to be consumed, but to be understood, to be transmuted. She was not just a guardian; she was a weaver, and the most intricate patterns were often born from the most chaotic threads. The choice had been made. Personal solace was a whisper in the wind; the greater responsibility was a roar that would echo through eternity. Her path was clear, forged in the crucible of sacrifice and illuminated by the enduring light of her lineage. She would not join her parents in their peace; she would fight to ensure that peace was possible for others.

The locket blazed with an inner fire, no longer a passive conduit but an active participant in the grand symphony of Elara's magic. The final sigil, a nexus of interlocking circles that seemed to encompass all of creation, responded to her touch with an unparalleled surge of energy. It wasn't merely the residual power of her ancestors, nor the raw, untamed might of the Shadow Lord's encroaching influence. This was Elara's own power, a nascent force that had lain dormant, waiting for the crucible of this moment to awaken. As her finger traced the last curve, the Sigil of Union, the chamber erupted in a blinding white light, so pure and intense it seemed to momentarily eclipse the very stars. The locket pulsed in her hand, a miniature sun resonating with the core of her being, and then, with a final, resonant thrum, the light subsided, leaving behind a profound and unwavering sense of stability.

The Veil, that ethereal shield woven from countless threads of magic and will, hummed with renewed vitality. The oppressive weight that had pressed down on the world, the insidious chill that had seeped into the very bones of reality, began to recede. It was not a violent expulsion, but a gentle, inexorable settling, like the tide turning after a fierce storm. The tendrils of darkness that had clawed at the edges of Elara's vision, the whispers of despair that had sought to undermine her resolve, now seemed distant, muted, like the fading echoes of a nightmare. The immediate threat, the palpable danger that had loomed over her since the moment she understood her inheritance, had been pushed back. Not vanquished, for such a concept was alien to the eternal dance between light and shadow, but undeniably held at bay, the balance restored, at least for now.

Kael watched, his ancient eyes reflecting the fading luminescence, a rare smile gracing his lips. He saw not just the completion of a ritual, but the awakening of a guardian. Elara, the orphan girl who had arrived at the Citadel a vessel of lineage, had now become its heart. The transformation was not merely in her command of magic, but in the very core of her spirit. The girl who had felt lost, adrift in a world that had taken everything from her, now stood as a beacon, her presence a promise of safety, her eyes reflecting a nascent power that spoke of resilience and unwavering purpose. She had not simply honored her parents' legacy; she had embraced it, weaving it into the fabric of her own burgeoning identity, forging something new and uniquely her own.

The locket, once a symbol of her inherited burden, now felt like an extension of her own will. Its warmth was no longer just a reminder of those who had come before, but a testament to the living strength that now resided within her. She could feel the Citadel's magical heart beating in tandem with her own, its ancient stones resonating with the power she now channeled. The years of arduous training, the moments of doubt and fear, the overwhelming weight of responsibility – all of it had culminated in this singular, defining moment. It was the end of her initial trial, a rite of passage that had tested her to her very limits, and the dawn of a new era, not just for her, but for the world she had sworn to protect.

Elara took a deep, steadying breath, the air in the chamber cleaner, lighter than it had been moments before. She looked down at her hands, still faintly tingling from the magic she had wielded. The raw power of the Shadow Lord had been an overwhelming force, a primal chaos that threatened to consume. Yet, she had not succumbed. Instead, she had learned to understand it, to see its place within the grand tapestry of existence, and to weave it, not to destroy, but to reinforce. It was a revelation that shifted her entire perspective on the nature of their struggle. The Shadow Lord was not an external enemy to be eradicated, but a force to be understood, managed, and ultimately, integrated into the balance. This understanding was the true gift of her lineage, a wisdom that transcended mere magical prowess.

"You have done it, Elara." Kael's voice was soft, carrying a profound reverence. "You have not only completed the Ritual of Sealing, but you have done so with a depth of understanding few Elder Weavers have ever achieved. The Veil is strong. The immediate darkness has receded."

Elara turned to face him, her gaze clear and steady. "But it is not gone," she stated, her voice firm with conviction. "The Shadow Lord is a constant. This is not an end, is it, Kael? It is a beginning."

Kael nodded slowly, his expression thoughtful. "Indeed. The Veil is a living tapestry, Elara. It requires constant tending, constant vigilance. Your parents understood this. They understood that the battle was not for a single victory, but for an eternal vigil. You have stepped into their shoes, but you have also forged your own path. You have taken their sacrifice and built upon it, transforming it from a final act into a foundation for continued protection."

The chamber, once alive with the volatile energies of the ritual, now pulsed with a serene, potent magic. The sigils on the altar glowed with a soft, steady light, their power a comforting presence rather than an overwhelming force. Elara could feel the Citadel responding to her, its ancient architecture humming with a resonance that mirrored her own. The very stones seemed to sigh with relief, their burden eased by her successful completion of the ritual. She had faced her deepest fears, confronted the seductive whispers of despair, and emerged not unscathed, but fundamentally changed. The orphan girl who had entered this chamber seeking answers had found a purpose, a destiny, and the strength to embrace it.

She could feel the subtle currents of the world beyond the Citadel's walls, the pulse of life that the Veil protected. It was a world that slept, unaware of the silent war waged on its behalf, a world that continued its cycles of joy and sorrow, of birth and death, under the shield of her lineage. This connection, this awareness of the vast, intricate web of life she now safeguarded, was an awe-inspiring and humbling realization. It solidified her resolve, transforming the abstract concept of duty into a deeply personal commitment.

"The locket," Elara murmured, her fingers tracing the cool, intricate patterns etched onto its surface. "It holds so much. Not just magic, but memories. Echoes of their love, their sacrifices. I felt them, Kael. In the vision. They were at peace."

"And that peace," Kael said, his voice gentle, "was earned through their vigilance. They gave their lives so that others might find that peace, not by escaping the world, but by defending it. You understood that, Elara. You chose to continue their work, to uphold the promise of their sacrifice. That is the true mark of an Elder Weaver."

The weight of her lineage felt less like a burden and more like a mantle, a symbol of trust bestowed upon her. She was no longer just Elara, the girl who had lost everything. She was Elara, the Elder Weaver, the guardian of the Veil, the inheritor of a sacred duty. The journey had been arduous, fraught with peril and doubt, but it had led her to this moment, this place of clarity and power. She had faced the darkness, both external and internal, and had emerged as a light.

"The Shadow Lord is not defeated," Elara said, her voice resonating with newfound authority. "The Veil is strong, but it will always be tested. This ritual is not the end of my training, but the beginning of my guardianship."

Kael inclined his head, his gaze filled with respect. "You are ready, Elara. The Citadel has accepted you. The Veil acknowledges you. You are no longer merely fulfilling a legacy; you are shaping it. This is the dawn of your era."

As Kael spoke, a subtle shift occurred within the chamber. The energies that had been so potent and volatile during the ritual began to coalesce, to settle into a harmonious, enduring hum. It was the sound of the Veil at its strongest, a constant, almost imperceptible thrum of protective magic that resonated through the very foundations of the Citadel. Elara could feel it seeping into the stone, into the air, into her own being. It was a feeling of profound belonging, of being intrinsically connected to this ancient bastion of power and to the world it sheltered.

She envisioned the Veil not as a static barrier, but as a dynamic, ever-evolving force, constantly responding to the ebb and flow of magical energies. Her role was not to simply maintain it, but to actively participate in its growth, to adapt it to the ever-changing threats that would inevitably arise. The Shadow Lord, in its ceaseless pursuit of dissolution, would always seek new ways to breach the defenses. Her understanding of its nature, her ability to weave its chaotic essence into the fabric of protection, would be her greatest asset.

Elara raised her hand, and the locket pulsed gently in response. She could feel the residual magic of the ritual swirling around her, a vibrant, protective aura. It was a tangible representation of her journey, of the girl who had been terrified of her own potential, now standing tall, ready to face whatever challenges lay ahead. The isolation she had once felt was replaced by a deep sense of connection, not just to her ancestors, but to all those who depended on the Veil for their safety and peace.

The whispers of the Shadow Lord had been silenced, but their memory served as a stark reminder of the ever-present danger. It was a lesson etched into her soul: vigilance was not a choice, but a necessity. Her parents had understood this, and their sacrifice was a testament to the unwavering commitment required of an Elder Weaver. They had fought not for an end to conflict, but for the opportunity for life to flourish, for peace to exist, however precariously.

As Elara looked around the chamber, no longer a place of fear and uncertainty, but a sanctuary of power and purpose, she felt a profound sense of gratitude. Gratitude for the lineage that had chosen her, for the mentors who had guided her, and for the inner strength that had finally bloomed within her. The journey had been one of immense personal growth, transforming an orphan girl into a beacon of hope, a guardian forged in the fires of ancient magic and unwavering resolve. The immediate trial was over, the Veil secured, but her path as an Elder Weaver had just begun. The dawning of this new era was not just for her, but for the world she now stood ready to protect, a world that could sleep soundly, knowing that its most sacred defense was in capable hands. Her own hands.

THE END...